Full House

"Those eight men would like nothing more than to put a bullet in you. That's eight bullets."

"One from each?" Clint asked. "How many of them do you think I'd take with me? I'm betting at least . . . five?"

"Are you that good?"

Clint smiled.

"There was a time I would have said six, but I was young then."

"And faster?"

"Dumber," Clint said, "more arrogant. No, five is an honest opinion."

"That wouldn't accomplish anything."

"What do you suggest?"

"Give me your gun. Walk over to the jail with me."

"And then what?"

"Tell your story to a jury."

"Go to trial?" Clint asked. "For something I didn't do? Kill a man I never met."

"They say their boss met with the Gunsmith."

"Or a man claiming to be the Gunsmith."

"Convince a jury of that," Yatesman said. "We can walk back to your poker game and talk to the judge."

"The judge doesn't want me in your jail."

"What makes you say that?"

Clint smiled again.

"I have most of his money."

DON'T MISS THESE ALL-ACTION WESTERN SERIES FROM THE BERKLEY PUBLISHING GROUP

THE GUNSMITH by J. R. Roberts

Clint Adams was a legend among lawmen, outlaws, and ladies. They called him . . . the Gunsmith.

LONGARM by Tabor Evans

The popular long-running series about Deputy U.S. Marshal Custis Long—his life, his loves, his fight for justice.

SLOCUM by Jake Logan

Today's longest-running action Western. John Slocum rides a deadly trail of hot blood and cold steel.

BUSHWHACKERS by B. J. Lanagan

An action-packed series by the creators of Longarm! The rousing adventures of the most brutal gang of cutthroats ever assembled—Quantrill's Raiders.

DIAMONDBACK by Guy Brewer

Dex Yancey is Diamondback, a Southern gentleman turned con man when his brother cheats him out of the family fortune. Ladies love him. Gamblers hate him. But nobody pulls one over on Dex . . .

WILDGUN by Jack Hanson

The blazing adventures of mountain man Will Barlow—from the creators of Longarm!

TEXAS TRACKER by Tom Calhoun

J.T. Law: the most relentless—and dangerous—manhunter in all Texas. Where sheriffs and posses fail, he's the best man to bring in the most vicious outlaws—for a price.

J. R. ROBERTS

JOVE BOOKS, NEW YORK

THE BERKLEY PUBLISHING GROUP
Published by the Penguin Group
Penguin Group (USA) Inc.
375 Hudson Street, New York, New York 10014, USA
Penguin Group (Canada), 90 Eglinton Avenue East, Suite 700, Toronto, Ontario M4P 2Y3, Canada
(a division of Pearson Penguin Canada Inc.)
Penguin Books Ltd. , 80 Strand, London WC2R 0RL, England
Penguin Group Ireland, 25 St. Stephen's Green, Dublin 2, Ireland (a division of Penguin Books Ltd.)
Penguin Group (Australia), 250 Camberwell Road, Camberwell, Victoria 3124, Australia
(a division of Pearson Australia Group Pty. Ltd.)
Penguin Books India Pvt. Ltd. , 11 Community Centre, Panchsheel Park, New Delhi—110 017, India
Penguin Group (NZ), 67 Apollo Drive, Rosedale, North Shore 0632, New Zealand
(a division of Pearson New Zealand Ltd.)
Penguin Books (South Africa) (Pty.) Ltd. , 24 Sturdee Avenue, Rosebank, Johannesburg 2196,
South Africa

Penguin Books Ltd. , Registered Offices: 80 Strand, London WC2R 0RL, England

THE TOWN COUNCIL MEETING

A Jove Book / published by arrangement with the author

PRINTING HISTORY
Jove edition / August 2009

Cover illustration by Sergio Giovine.

For information, address: The Berkley Publishing Group,
a division of Penguin Group (USA) Inc.,
375 Hudson Street, New York, New York 10014.

ISBN: 978-0-515-14664-6

JOVE®
Jove Books are published by The Berkley Publishing Group,
a division of Penguin Group (USA) Inc.,
375 Hudson Street, New York, New York 10014.
JOVE® is a registered trademark of Penguin Group (USA) Inc.
The "J" design is a trademark of Penguin Group (USA) Inc.

PRINTED IN THE UNITED STATES OF AMERICA

10 9 8 7 6 5 4 3 2 1

ONE

Clint was in a café when he heard all the commotion outside. He picked up his mug of coffee and carried it outside with him. About eight riders had come storming into town, kicking up dust and scattering people. Folks were coming out from their homes and businesses to see what the ruckus was about.

"What's going on?" he asked a man with an apron who was standing near him. He had come out of the general store next to the café.

"Don't rightly know," the man said. "Those boys are from the Bar K ranch, though."

"Big outfit?" Clint asked.

"Not the biggest, but big enough," the man replied. "Looks like they're goin' into the sheriff's office."

"Well," Clint said, "none of my business."

He took his cup back inside and asked the waitress for some more.

Clint had been in Cannon City, Wyoming, for three days. The food at this small café wasn't the best, but the coffee was. He'd go a long way for a good cup of coffee, and they served a nice little breakfast to go with it.

The waitress was also the prettiest girl he'd seen since arriving in town. Well, actually, she was more woman than girl, probably about thirty. She flirted with him, but he'd seen her flirt with other customers. He also found out early—and better early than never—that she was married to the cook.

So he went there for the coffee and to watch her walk around and serve customers.

At the moment, though, he was the only customer in the place. She poured him some more coffee, then put the pot down on the table and went to stare out the window.

"Somethin' awful must've happened out at the Bar K," she said. "Usually, those boys are avoidin' the sheriff, not visitin' him."

Is that unusual?" Clint asked. "Trouble out at the Bar K?"

"No, she answered, "but like I said, those boys are usually causin' the trouble."

"Well," Clint said, "I'm sure the sheriff can handle it. Him and his deputies."

"What deputies?" she asked. "This is a small town. It's just Sheriff Yatesman."

"In a small town news travels fast," Clint said. "I'm sure it'll make its way to you, soon."

Clint finished his coffee and paid the check, then put his hat on and stepped outside. As he did a bunch of men came pouring out of the sheriff's office, followed by the sheriff himself. They all mounted up and went riding out of town as hell-bent for leather as they had ridden in.

Somebody's dead, Clint thought.

* * *

Later, Clint was in Cannon City's smallest saloon. He liked it better than the other two because it was quiet. It was possible to play poker without having to listen to bad piano playing, bad singing, and drunken cowboys shouting back and forth. The other two saloons never had any poker games going.

He was in a five-handed game, not high stakes, but not penny ante, either. He was far enough ahead to make the game worth it. The other players were regulars, four men from town who always had room for a fifth, stranger or not.

Clint was staring down at a full house when the batwings swung inward and the doorway belched men into the room. He was facing the door so he saw them—the sheriff and the men from the Bar K.

"There he is!" someone shouted, pointing.

"Easy," the sheriff said. "Just stay here."

The ranch hands were obviously agitated, but they remained behind and went to the bar. They shoved several men out of the way and ordered drinks.

The sheriff walked over to the poker table.

"Clint Adams?"

Clint didn't look up.

"That's me."

"Can I talk to you?"

Now Clint looked at the man.

"Talk."

"Privately."

"I'm in the middle of a game, Sheriff," Clint said. "In fact, in the middle of a hand."

"Finish the hand, then," the sheriff said.

"You taking me in, Sheriff?"

"Not even takin' you to my office, Mr. Adams. We can talk here, at an empty table."

Clint thought it over, then said, "Okay. Get yourself a drink and wait for me at an empty table. I'll finish up this hand."

The sheriff stood there for a moment, then turned and went to the bar.

At the bar Arnold Coleman watched the sheriff walk to the bar.

"You gonna let him get away with that?" he asked.

"You see who he's playin' poker with?" the sheriff asked. "The judge, and the mayor, and two members of the town council."

"We don't care," Coleman said. He was the spokesman for the group. "If you're not gonna do your job, we will."

"All eight of you?" the sheriff asked. "Which one of you is gonna take the lead? Put a gun on the Gunsmith? Huh?"

The seven men behind Coleman looked away.

"That's what I thought," the lawman said. "Just stay here and let me do my job." He looked at the bartender. "Gimme a beer, Sammy."

The bartender set a full mug on the bar. The sheriff grabbed it and walked to an empty table.

TWO

Clint took the hand with a full house, then excused himself from the game. He walked over and sat opposite the sheriff. He still had full view of the room, especially the eight nervous men at the bar.

"Don't want a drink?" the sheriff asked.

"I think I'd make your nervous friends even more nervous if I went to the bar," Clint said. "What's this all about?"

"Do you know Big Ed Kennedy?"

"Big Ed?" Clint asked. "Is he a big guy?"

"He's a big man in this part of Wyoming," the sheriff said. "At least, he was until this mornin'."

"And what happened this morning?"

"Somebody killed him."

"I'm sorry to hear it," Clint said. "What's this got to do with me?"

"Big Ed told his foreman, Arnie Coleman, that he was hiring the Gunsmith."

"For what?"

"What else? For his gun."

"Why did Big Ed need a gun for hire?" Clint asked.

"He's havin' some trouble with some other ranchers in the area."

"A range war?" Clint asked. "There hasn't been a range war in years."

"These men have never stopped. You met Ed Kennedy. You know how old he is."

"Nice try, Sheriff," Clint said. "I never met Mr. Kennedy."

"Well, him and the other big ranchers around here—Matt Holmes and Andy Rivers—are all in their seventies."

"Really? Are they healthy old fellows?"

"All but Big Ed," the sheriff said. "He's dead."

"And let me guess," Clint said. "I'm supposed to have killed him? A man I never met?"

"Who says you never met him?"

"Who says I did?"

"His men."

Clint looked over at them.

"All of them? Or one of them, and the other seven are simply agreeing?"

"Those eight men would like nothing more than to put a bullet in you. That's eight bullets."

"One from each?" Clint asked. "How many of them do you think I'd take with me? I'm betting at least . . . five?"

"Are you that good?"

Clint smiled.

"There was a time I would have said six, but I was young then."

"And faster?"

"Dumber," Clint said, "more arrogant. No, five is an honest opinion."

"That wouldn't accomplish anything."

"What do you suggest?"

"Give me your gun. Walk over to the jail with me."

"And then what?"

"Tell your story to a jury."

"Go to trial?" Clint asked. "For something I didn't do? Kill a man I never met."

"They say their boss met with the Gunsmith."

"Or a man claiming to be the Gunsmith."

"Convince a jury of that," Yatesman said. "We can walk back to your poker game and talk to the judge."

"The judge doesn't want me in your jail."

"What makes you say that?"

Clint smiled again.

"I have most of his money."

THREE

"Okay," Yatesman said, "how about this? You keep your gun but take a walk over to my office with me."

"I still don't know why I'd do that, Sheriff."

"Well, what do you want to do?"

"If I had my druthers? I'd go back to my poker game, finish it, have something to eat. Go back to my hotel, get a good night's sleep, and ride out of this town come morning. End of story."

"But it wouldn't be the end of the story," the lawman said. "Those men would hunt you down."

"You think so?"

"Oh yes," Yatesman said. "You see, Big Ed's men loved him. So I think they'd come after you, and there would be more than eight of them. They got at least twenty men working out there. You want to take on twenty mad ranch hands?"

"I don't want to take on anybody, Sheriff," Clint said. "But I didn't kill Ed Kennedy, and I never met him."

The sheriff shook his head. He looked to be about forty-five or so, was probably a career lawman who thought he'd found himself a soft spot here to finish out his career.

Clint wasn't deliberately trying to be difficult. Well, maybe he was, but the fact remained he didn't give himself much of a chance if he gave up his gun and allowed himself to be locked in a cell. If Big Ed's men loved him the way the sheriff said they did, he'd be a dead man for sure. It was only the gun on his hip—and the sheriff—that was keeping them from coming after him.

"I need somebody smarter than me to figure this out," the sheriff said. "How about I invite the judge over here to help?"

"The judge is smarter than you?"

Yatesman shrugged. "He's a judge."

"I hope he's a better judge than he is a poker player," Clint said. "Go ahead. Invite him."

Clint sat back and watched the lawman walk to the poker game and speak to the judge, whose name—Clint had heard during the game—was Curtis. He didn't know if it was a first or last name, and he'd heard it only once. The other men at the table simply called him "Judge," just like they called the mayor "Mayor."

The judge frowned, snapped at the sheriff, then pushed his chair back and walked over with the lawman in tow.

He was in his sixties, wearing a dark suit that made his snow-white shirt and hair stand out. He sat down opposite Clint in the seat the sheriff had vacated. The lawman sat in a third chair.

"I kinda wish you'd told me I was playing poker with the Gunsmith, Adams," he said.

"Nobody exactly told me I was playing with a judge and a mayor," Clint said. "I had to hear it for myself during the game. Besides, the only thing that matters during a poker game is the cards."

The judge looked at Yatesman and said, "He's got that right."

"Judge, we got a problem," the sheriff said.

"Ain't that what we hired you for, Pete?"

"Well, Judge, I figure I'm doin' my job right now keepin' those eight ranch hands from shootin' up this saloon tryin' to get to Adams."

"Yeah, I noticed them come in. They don't look happy. Big Ed's men?"

"That's right."

"And what are they so mad about?"

"Big Ed's dead."

"Oh," the judge said. "That's too bad. And they think Adams killed him?"

"Yes, sir."

The judge looked at Adams.

"Didja?"

"No, sir."

"Can you prove it?"

"Don't know that I have to, Judge."

Now the judge looked at Yatesman.

"What exactly is the problem you want me to address, Pete?"

"Well . . . Adams won't come along peaceable.

"You got evidence that says he killed Ed Kennedy?" the jurist asked.

"Well, not exactly."

"What do you have, Sheriff?"

Yatesman told the judge he'd ridden out to the house, saw Big Ed in his house where his foreman had found him, shot. He and some of the hands had heard the shot and had come running. The foreman, Arnie Coleman, said the old man had told him he was going to hire the Gunsmith to clear up the trouble between him and his fellow ranchers.

"And did he?" the judge asked.

"I don't know, Judge."

"Son, did Big Ed try to hire you?"

"I've never met Big Ed, Judge," Clint said. "If he wanted to hire me, I didn't know anything about it. Maybe he made that decision when he heard I was in town."

"But he never sent for you?"

"No, sir."

"Pete, anybody see Adams out there?"

"Well, no . . ."

"Judge," Clint said, "what if one of the other ranchers heard that Kennedy wanted to hire me and sent in a man pretending to be me to kill Kennedy when they were alone?"

The judge looked at Yatesman.

"That make sense to you, Sheriff?"

"It's possible, I guess, but Adams can't prove that."

"T'aint his job to prove it," the judge said. "It's yours. I suggest you get those ranch hands out of here and go find some evidence before you try to arrest this man."

"But, Judge," Yatesman said, "I'm just barely holdin' those men back. I think Mr. Adams would be safer in my jail."

The judge looked at Clint.

"What do you think of that suggestion, son?" he asked.

"I think it stinks," Clint said. "In a cell with no gun I'd be a dead man."

"I agree with him, Peter," the judge said. "Move those men out of here."

"What if they won't go?"

"Then arrest every last one of 'em!" the judge said impatiently.

"You know," Yatesman said, standing up, "this is exactly why I been askin' for the money to hire me some deputies."

"Is that a fact?" the judge asked. "Well, there's the mayor over there. Why don't you ask him for the money? In fact, why don't you just bring the whole dang poker game over here to this table so we can have a damned town council meetin' on the subject right now?"

Yatesman stared at the judge for a few moments, until he realized the man wasn't being serious.

"Awww . . ." he said, turned and walked to the men at the bar.

"Thanks, Judge," Clint said.

"Don't thank me, young feller," the man said. "I'm only sidin' with you on this because you've got all my money. If it wasn't for that, I'd be sidin' with the law."

"Why?" Clint asked. "The law's got no right to put me in a cell."

"The law's got every right to do what it wants if I say so," the judge said.

"Well then, if you did that, you'd be putting the sheriff into an awful position."

"How's that?"

"He'd have to try to take my gun from me."

"And you'd resist?"

"I would."

"And those eight men tried to gun ya here and now, you'd fight back?"

"I would," Clint said.

"You'd get killed."

"So would a lot of them," Clint said, "and so would a lot of innocent people—maybe you, or the mayor. Maybe both. That wouldn't be very good for the town, would it?"

"Blast the town," the judge said. "It wouldn't be so damn good for me, neither."

They both looked over at the bar. The men were protesting, but it looked as if the sheriff was getting them closer to the door.

"You up for continuing our game?" the judge asked.

"Sure, why not? If you're not afraid of catching a stray piece of lead."

"I'm more afraid of not gettin' my money back."

Both men stood up and walked back to the poker game, reclaimed their seats.

"Damn well about time," the mayor said. "This feller's got all my money, Judge, and I can't get it back if the two of you are gonna go off and—"

"Gents," the judge said, cutting the mayor off, "I think I've got a mighty good reason for suggestin' we raise the stakes a little."

FOUR

They raised the stakes, and while they played the judge relayed the little problem they seemed to have to the other players. At the same time he introduced Clint to the other men.

"That sour-lookin' feller is our mayor, Walter Patton. We all just call him Mayor. That feller is Delbert Chambers, and this here is Ben Lawson. Ben, what do you do?"

"I open for ten," Lawson said.

"Call," the judge said. "The four of us have been in this town for over thirty years. In fact, the four of us pretty much built this town and we been the town council all these years."

"Are you a real judge?" Clint asked. "I raise."

"That I am, son," the judge said. "My name's Curtis."

"Judge Curtis? No first name?"

The man grinned around a slim cigar.

"My first name's Judge," he said, "and any man at this table tried to say different will have to deal with me."

The other three men said nothing.

"Delbert, there, he's a lawyer. Delbert, what do you do?"

"Call."

"Mayor?"

"I call."

"And Ben, he's a bookkeeper. Keeps the town's books, among others. Ben?" the judge asked.

"I call."

"So we're sittin' here playin' poker with the Gunsmith," Delbert Chambers said, "while there are eight angry men outside wantin' to pump him full of lead?"

"That's about the size of it."

"Goddamn it," Ben Lawson said, "if I was thirty years younger and fifty pounds lighter, I'd get the hell out of this chair and outta the line of fire."

In fact, Clint noticed that all four men were in their sixties and—except for the mayor—were carrying plenty of extra weight around their middles.

"Can I ask you gents something?" Clint asked.

"You can if we can keep playin' while you ask," Chambers said. "I'll take three cards, Judge."

The judge dealt him three.

"Did you all know Ed Kennedy?" Clint asked. "And the other ranchers he was fighting with? I'll take two."

"Oh hell, yes," the mayor answered. "We all know each other. Those old bastards have been fighting for years."

"Friendly rivals," Clint asked, "or would one of them hire a gunman to kill the other?"

"In a heartbeat," Chambers said. "Only reason they're not tryin' to kill each other is they're too old to get on a horse anymore. Too old to go out in a blaze of glory. Yeah, they'd hire it done."

"You sure Big Ed didn't try to hire you?" Lawson asked. "Two cards."

"I'm sure," Clint said. "I have never met the man."

"Sure seems funny," Chambers said.

"Whaddaya gonna do, Adams?" Lawson asked.

"I'm going to sit here and play poker."

"Pretty brave," Mayor Patton said. "I was you, I'd get on my horse and get out of this town—this county. I'll take one card."

"I walk out that door somebody's liable to take a shot at me," Clint said. "Right now I'm safer in here, sitting with you gents. I don't figure anybody's going to want to shoot up the town council."

All four men laughed and the judge said, "You've never been to one of our meetings."

"Folks are yellin' at us all the time," Delbert Chambers said.

"Take a shot at one of us in a minute, if they thought they could get away with it," Ben Lawson said, chuckling.

"Well," Clint said, "somebody took a shot at Ed Kennedy and it wasn't me. I'm going to sit right here until I can figure a safe way out."

"Well, I gotta tell ya," Chambers said, "I agree with you. You go into a cell without your gun and you're a dead man. I bet twenty."

"Naw," Lawson said, "be best to put yourself in the sheriff's care until he can find out who killed Big Ed."

"And what if everybody just decides that I did it?" Clint asked.

"Well then," Lawson said, "Delbert here would defend you in the judge's court."

"And the judge would listen to all the evidence and decide whether or not you should go to trial," Chambers said.

"I call," was all the judge said.

Clint looked around the table. He sure hoped all of these men were better at their jobs than they were at poker.

"Sorry," Clint said, "I pass."

"In this hand?" Chambers asked.

"On putting myself in the sheriff's care."

"Can't blame you for that," Mayor Patton said.

"Don't start that again," the judge said.

"Start what?" Clint asked. "I raise twenty."

"Fold," Lawson said. "Our esteemed mayor doesn't think Yatesman's doin' the job. He's been wantin' to replace the man for a long time."

"And why haven't you?"

"Can't fire him without a majority vote of the council," Patton said. "I call."

"And there isn't one?"

"No," Chambers said. "Call. I think Yatesman's doin' his job."

"I call," the judge said.

"Full house," Clint said.

"Again?" Chambers complained, throwing his two pair down.

"Maybe we should put Mr. Adams in a cell," Lawson said.

"Not while he's got my money," the judge said. He looked at Clint. "Deal."

FIVE

"Why don't we offer Adams, here, the job?" Lawson asked.

"What job?" Clint asked, shuffling the cards.

"Sheriff," Lawson said. "You fellas can't tell me you wouldn't rather have the Gunsmith as sheriff instead of Pete Yatesman."

"Pete Yatesman wouldn't attract gunslingers to town," Chambers said. "Adams would."

"And are you proposing he investigates his own involvement in Ed Kennedy's death?" Patton asked.

"Hold on," Clint said. "I've got something to say about this. I am not involved in Ed Kennedy's death, and I don't want the job as sheriff."

He dealt out the cards for another hand of draw poker.

"Doesn't matter what you say, son," the judge commented. "The word is out there. There's folks who are gonna believe you did it."

"What the hell kind of system of justice is that?" Clint asked.

"That's the only one we got in town," the judge said. "Come on, Ben, don't make us ask you every time."

"I open for five . . ."

It was late afternoon and Clint was getting hungry.

"They serve food in this saloon?" he asked the table.

"Nope," Chambers said.

"We can send out for somethin', though," the judge said. "I mean, if you just don't want to leave the saloon."

"Yeah," Patton said, "then we can keep playin'."

"That sounds good," Clint said.

"Sandwiches okay?" the judge asked.

"Sandwiches are fine."

"Sammy?" the judge shouted.

The bartender came running.

"Yeah, Judge."

"Where's Joby?"

"In the back."

"Send him to the café for some sandwiches."

"What kind, Judge?"

The judge looked at Clint.

"All kinds," he said.

"You heard the man."

"Yes, sir."

"Okay," the judge said, "who deals?"

Half an hour later a boy about ten came in carrying a wicker basket. He carried it to the poker table.

"Thank you, Joby," the judge said.

"You got to pay," Joby said.

"Mr. Adams," the judge said, "since you're the only one ahead, how about you buy lunch for the table?"

"It'd be my pleasure."

He gave the boy the money for the food, then tipped him four bits.

"Thanks, mister!"

The kid ran out.

"Great," Patton said, "now we'll have to do that all the time."

"You ruined him," Lawson said.

"Hey," Clint said, "even a kid's got to make a livin'."

They left the basket on the floor and passed sandwiches around. Clint ended up with meat loaf. It was better than anything he'd had at the café, except for breakfast.

While they were eating the batwings opened and the sheriff walked in. He came right to the table.

"Hey, Sheriff," the judge said. "Have a sandwich?"

"Don't mind if I do." He bent over, pulled out a sandwich. Turkey.

"Sammy?" the judge shouted.

"Yeah, Judge."

"Five beers."

"Comin' up."

"Thanks, Judge," the sheriff said.

"Don't thank me," the judge said. "Thank Mr. Adams. He's buyin' lunch."

The sheriff stopped chewing, then shrugged and continued. The bartender came over with the five beers and set them on the table.

Clint said, "I guess you better start me a tab, Sammy."

The bartender looked at the judge, who nodded.

"Sure thing," the barman said and went back to the bar.

"What's on your mind, Sheriff?" the judge asked.

"I, uh, came to talk to Adams."

"So, talk," the judge said. "We can play while you talk."

Yatesman looked around the table.

"Everybody here knows what's goin' on," the judge said. "Just consider this a town council meeting."

Yatesman thought about it, bit into his sandwich, and said, "Yeah, okay."

SIX

"They're gonna come into town later this afternoon," the sheriff said.

"Who is?" Clint asked.

"The men from the Bar K."

"How many?"

"All of 'em," Yatesman said. "I ain't gonna be able to stop twenty men."

"You better," the judge said.

"What?"

The judge looked up at him.

"Joby!" he shouted.

"Yeah, Judge."

"Run to my office and get my gavel."

"Yes, sir."

The boy ran out.

"Judge—" the sheriff said.

"Wait."

They played a hand while Joby was gone. The judge won it.

"Hey," he said, raking in the money, "tide's gonna turn."

Joby came in and gave the judge his gavel.

"Wait, boy."

He slammed the gavel down on the table.

"Here," he said to Joby, "put it back."

"Yes, sir."

The judge looked up at the sheriff.

"This is now an official meeting of the town council, Sheriff," he said. "It's your duty to see that we're not disturbed."

"Against twenty men?" Yatesman asked. "With no deputies?"

The judge looked around the table.

"All right, gents, pony up."

"Huh?" Chambers asked.

"Ten dollars each should do it."

"For what?" Lawson asked.

"Come on, come on," the judge said. He took out a ten and put it on the table. The other men followed, placing a ten on top until there were four—and then Clint reached over and laid down a fifth.

"Obliged," the judge said.

He picked up the fifty dollars and handed it to the sheriff.

"Hire yourself some deputies," he said.

"Temporary one," Patton added. "Just until this thing is over."

"Don't if anybody's gonna volunteer, when they hear what's happening."

"Don't wait for volunteers," the judge said. "Now go on."

The sheriff picked up his beer, drank half of it, and then left.

"Nice move, Judge," Mayor Patton said. "Now whose deal is it?"

A couple of hours later the sheriff returned. The judge had just lost a hand he was sure was his. He'd had as full house, but he lost when Clint dropped his cards on the table, revealing four threes.

To their credit, as Clint continued to win, these four men never made a comment about cheating. To a man they realized they were being outplayed. They didn't like it, but they respected it.

"Goddamn, man," the judge said. "We're getting' a lesson today."

"And payin' for it," Patton said.

"You fellas want to call it a day?" Clint asked.

"Hell no," Chambers said. "Deal 'em."

The judge looked up at the sheriff.

"What now?"

"I got my deputies."

"Good."

"I got three," Yatesman said. "You wanna know who they are?"

"No, I don't wanna know who they are," the judge said. "Just make sure they keep the Bar K boys out of here."

"Out of the saloon, completely?" Yatesman asked.

"That's what I said. What did you think you were hirin' them for?"

"Well . . . to keep the peace. Keep them from shooting at Adams."

"And you can do that by keepin' them the hell out of here," the judge said. "You understand that?"

"Yes, sir."

"Good."

"I'll position them in the front and the back of the building."

"How you deploy them is up to you, Sheriff," the judge said.

Yatesman looked at Clint, who gave him no sympathy. He was still trying to figure a way out of the situation. He considered sneaking out the back, retrieving Eclipse from the livery, and getting out of town, but by doing that he could end up being a wanted man. The unfairness of the situation kept growing.

"One thing, Sheriff," Clint said.

"What's that?"

"My horse," Clint said. "He's in the livery. If anything happens to him, I'm not going to be happy."

"Your horse?" Yatesman said. "I can't have a man watching your horse."

"Put the animal somewhere safe," the judge said.

"Judge," the sheriff said, "if this man is guilty of murder—"

"You don't have any evidence of that, yet, do you?" the judge asked, cutting him off.

"No, I don't."

"Well then, don't talk to me about it until you do. Now get out, you're interrupting our meeting."

"Come on, Judge, this ain't a real meeting—"

"Were you here when I banged my gavel?"

"Well, yeah, but—"

"And do you see a majority of the town council seated at this table?"

"Yeah . . ."

"And ain't we been discussing town business, gents?" the judge asked.

"Oh yeah," Lawson said, "we been discussing whether or not we should replace our sheriff."

"What?"

"So far," the judge said, "I'm against it."

"Judge—"

"But you never know, Pete," the judge said, gathering up his cards, "you just never know."

SEVEN

The game continued, with all the players seemingly unconcerned about what was happening outside. In fact, Clint was very interested in just how effective the sheriff and his drafted deputies were going to be in keeping the Bar K boys out of the saloon. If twenty men came in with their guns blazing, he was just one of the people who was going to end up dead.

Business was picking up in the saloon, and the poker game was starting to attract some attention. Also, the saloon girls who worked the floor had started working to sell drinks. The place was filling up with the people, and gunfire would mean panic and death.

"Adams?" the judge said. "The play is to you, son. You with us?"

"I am, Judge," Clint said. "I call."

At the bar two men started arguing. Nobody knew what they were arguing about—least of all them—because they were so drunk they weren't making any sense.

"Those two idiots are gonna start shootin' at each other

soon," Ben Lawson said. "Where the hell's the law when you need him?"

"I think our good sheriff is pretty occupied at the moment, Ben," Patton said.

"Well, somebody ought to do somethin'," Chambers said. "Those two idiots have taken their guns out."

"For chrissake," the judge said, "if you're both so worried walk over there and disarm them. They're just a couple harmless drunks."

"Well," Lawson said, "those guns look pretty deadly to me."

"Adams," the judge said, "would you mind doin' somethin'?"

"My pleasure," Clint said, "if only to shut you all up about it."

He half turned and drew his gun.

"Look out!" somebody yelled.

The two drunks did, indeed, have their guns out and trained on each other, and if Clint didn't do something soon somebody was sure to get hurt.

Clint had a clear field of fire so he pulled the trigger on his gun twice.

Everybody was shocked to see the two drunk's guns leap out of their hands, but nobody was more surprised than the two men themselves.

Clint ejected the spent shells, replaced them, and holstered the gun. He didn't like showing off, but this was a special situation. Word might get outside the building about what he'd done. Maybe it would change the mind of some of the ranch hands who were waiting to kill him and send them scurrying back to the ranch.

"Now either get out or keep it quiet," Clint shouted at the two men.

"Yes, sir," they both said and turned back to their drinks. They needed them now.

"Thanks, Adams," the judge said.

"See?" Lawson said. "This is the man who should be sheriff."

"Knock it off, Lawson," Clint said. "I'm not looking for a job."

"Wearing a badge hereabouts might just keep you from gettin' shot," Chambers pointed out.

"Mr. Chambers," Clint said, "in my experience nothing makes a bigger target out of a man than pinning a badge on."

"How about a reputation?" the judge asked.

Clint looked at the man and said, "I open."

EIGHT

Jennifer O'Dell brought a tray of drinks to the table, something for everyone but Clint.

"I take it you don't drink during a poker game," the judge said. "I noticed you only had enough beer with lunch to wash it down."

"That's right, Judge," Clint said. "If you get drunk during a game, it tends to make you brave . . ."

"Don't you need to be brave to win big?" Ben Lawson asked.

"Maybe in the practice of the law that's true," Clint said. "Mostly, in big games, you need to be brave just to play. You need to be in control to win." He looked up at Jennifer. "Can you bring me a cup of coffee?"

"Sure thing, Clint," she said.

All five men watched the girl walk to the bar. Of course, Clint had been doing more than just watching her since he got to town. He'd spotted her the first night, and she'd been ready to be swept off her feet by a stranger in town.

She brought him his coffee and leaned over to breathe in his ear.

"Your room tonight?"

"No, sweetie," he said, "yours—but we'll have to be quick. I think this meeting is going to go on all night."

She breathed in his ear again and left. Clint lifted his eyes to see all for men looking at him.

"Is it to me?" he asked.

"That girl won't give any of the men in this town the time of day," Ben Lawson said.

"Have you tried, Ben?" Clint asked.

"Not me," Lawson said. "I'm too old."

"What have you got that the men in this town ain't got?" Chambers asked.

"Maybe that's it," Clint said.

"What's it?" Patton asked.

"I don't live in town," he said. "She won't have to see me after the next few days."

"You might be dead within the next few days."

"But I won't be dead tonight," Clint said.

"Hey," the judge said, "we said we was gonna play all night."

"We ain't never played in an all-night game before," Chambers said.

"Well, gents, in an all-night game it's very important to be relaxed," Clint said, "and to take breaks."

"Breaks?" Mayor Patton asked.

"Yes," Clint said. "You don't have to leave the building, but a break to refresh yourself is very important."

"Refresh?" Patton asked. "You said not to drink."

"He means wash your face and hands, Mayor," the judge said.

"Oh yeah," the mayor said, "refresh."

Only to Clint, "refresh" meant a little bit more than that.

* * *

The first night with Jennifer had been frenzied. If the town council was right, then she had not had sex in some time. She came to Clint's room eager for it, pushing him inside when he answered the door and fairly ripping his clothes off. Luckily, he had already removed his boots, so she'd been able to pull his pants off quickly.

The moment his erect penis came into view her eyes lit up and she said, "Yessss!"

"I hope it's okay," he said. "What you expected?"

"Oh yes," she said, wrapping both hands around it. "I knew it would be . . . beautiful."

She rubbed it against her breasts, enjoying the heat of it, the smoothness of the skin, then rubbed it against her mouth. Finally, she licked her lips and then took his inside. He gasped as the heat of her mouth engulfed him, and she began to suck him wetly. Now that he knew it had been a long time for her, he understood why she spent so much time sucking on him. He was just glad that he'd been able to show some stamina and stay with her.

Because he'd never had his cock sucked for so long in his life, or with such . . . fervor . . .

"Adams?"

Clint looked at the judge.

"Yes?"

"Your deal."

"Gents," Clint said, "remember what I said about taking a break?"

"Yeah."

"I think we should take one," he said.

"Why?" the mayor asked.

"Because I'm tired," Clint said, "and I can only wonder how you fellows feel."

"You sayin' that because we're older than you?" Ben Lawson demanded.

Clint smiled.

"I'm saying that because you fellows were playing long before I got here, weren't you?"

"He's right about that," the mayor said.

"Also," Clint said, standing up and addressing the judge, "I'm sure you want to check on the progress outside."

"I suppose I should," the judge said. "All right. How long a break?"

Clint looked over at Jennifer, sighed, and said, "I guess about an hour should do it."

When he and Jennifer got into her room she said, "Only an hour?"

"Well, honey," he said, "I am playing poker with the town council, you know. Those are important men."

"Not as important as they think they are," she said. "Okay, give me five minutes to freshen up."

He grabbed her and said, "I like you dirty."

"I'm not dirty," she said, pushing him away, "but I am a little smelly. Be patient."

As she went to wash up he took the opportunity to walk to the window and look out at the street. The ranch hands were still out there. They had torches going, which kept the street lighted. He could see them standing around, waiting for the word to go in.

From his vantage point he could not see the sheriff and his new deputies, but they must have been out there or the men would have charged into the saloon a long time ago.

Clint wondered who had killed Big Ed Kennedy. It certainly wasn't him, but he could understand why his men thought it was. It was part of carrying around a big reputation with a gun.

He thought it was likely someone had impersonated him, either to defraud the rancher of a lot of money or just to get him alone and kill him. If the point was to kill him, then the man was probably hired by one of the other ranchers.

Clint's inclination was to look into the matter himself and clear his name. But that would make it necessary for him to leave the saloon. These men were sure to gun him down at first sight.

"Clint?"

He turned.

"How do I look?"

She had put on a filmy nightgown, which showed off her long legs and her large breasts.

"Oh my," he said.

She smiled, pleased at his reaction.

NINE

As much as he liked her nightgown he walked to her and pulled it down from her shoulders. Her full breasts bobbed into view and he took their weight into his hands, brushing her large nipples with his thumbs. He lifted them to his mouth and sucked the nipples in turn, squeezing them at the same time. She moaned but pulled away so she could sink to her knees.

She pulled open Clint's pants and reached inside for him. Her fingers wrapped around his hard shaft and freed his cock so she could get a look at it. Gazing at him hungrily, she opened her mouth and placed her lips upon the tip of his penis and slid her tongue against the smooth, sensitive skin.

Clint felt his knees buckle slightly as she eased her lips all the way down to take him completely inside her mouth. He knew he was in for more of the same as the first night they'd been together, but he didn't have that much time. He was about to pull away when she ran her tongue up and down the bottom of his cock, teasing the sensitive spot right beneath the head. In moments he was rock hard and ready to explode.

Grabbing her shoulders, Clint eased her back so he could collect himself. She looked up at him and immediately leaned in to suck him some more. It felt so good he didn't want it to stop, but somehow, he managed to keep control. Clint took hold of her and moved her toward the bed.

He pushed her into her back and got rid of his clothes. Joining her on the bed he got between her legs and touched the tip of his erect penis to her wet slit. He pushed in easily and she gasped. Once he was all the way inside of her he grabbed her by the hips as she let out a gasp of pleasure and closed her eyes tightly.

But Jennifer wanted to be on top, and Clint decided to let her. Fighting her might take too long. He let her flip him over, and her knees dropped down on either side of him. She supported herself by placing both hands flat upon his chest. She started to ride him in earnest, tossing her head back and giving herself up to the moment.

Clint pawed her breasts, pinched her nipples, ran his hands up and down her strong back and over her almost-chubby thighs. She lay down on top of him, then, crushing her breasts against him, brought her hips into action and lifted her butt up and down faster and faster until the sound of slapping flesh filled the room.

"Yes," she shouted, "oh yes, like that, right there, oh, right there . . . don't stop . . ."

But she was in control, and stopping was within her purview—and she wasn't about to. He felt as if his cock were elongating, getting deeper and deeper inside of her every time she came down on him. She was so wet it was running down his thighs, and the room filled with the sweet scent of her.

Finally she jammed herself down on him tightly. He

could feel her entire body go taut for a moment, and then she was flopping about on top of him as if she'd lost control of her body.

Hurriedly, he flipped her over without breaking contact with her and began to fuck her for all he was worth, chasing his own release, trying to achieve before hers could fade away. She gasped and moaned as he slammed into her, and then she began to ride another wave just as he felt the build up in his legs and thighs and then suddenly he was exploding inside of her. She started shouting and finally bit into his shoulder to keep herself from screaming.

He wondered if anyone downstairs or outside could hear her—but he didn't really care. It would certainly let them know that he wasn't in there, worrying about anything else that was going on outside.

TEN

Back at the table the other four men—the town council—were already waiting. They watched him as he walked across the room and sat down.

"Rested?" the judge asked.

"Oh yes," Clint said. "You?"

"Somewhat refreshed."

"Whose deal is it?" Clint asked.

"It's Ben's," the mayor said.

Delbert Chambers leaned forward and asked, "Ain't you the least bit worried about what's goin' on outside?"

"Well," Clint said, "I'd say I was interested, but not exactly worried."

"I'd be worried," Lawson said, while he shuffled the cards, "if twenty men or so were outside waitin' to kill me."

"If I was that worried," Clint said, "I'd have to stop playing because I wouldn't be able to concentrate on what I was doing—which, in this case, is taking money from you gents."

"I figure the tide will turn," the judge said.

"Yeah," Mayor Patton added, "if he stays alive long enough."

"Deal the cards, Ben," Clint said. "Judge, you got something you want to tell me?"

"Well, yeah," the judge said. "I talked to the sheriff and this is what he told me happened a little while ago . . ."

Out in front of the saloon Sheriff Yatesman stared out at the men in the street—all holding burning torches and all wearing guns. He didn't know what he'd do if they suddenly tossed the torches through the window of the saloon.

"What do we do," one of his new deputies asked, "if they decide to throw those torches through the window of the saloon?"

Yatesman looked at the man.

"Shoot anybody who does that," he said.

"Yes, sir."

"Sheriff," another deputy said, "I ain't gettin' paid enough to shoot anybody."

"Any of you has to shoot somebody you'll get another ten dollars."

"That suits me," the first man said. "And it'll suit my brother, too." His brother was around the back, keeping watch. He had a shotgun and was supposed to fire it if anyone tried to get into the saloon that way.

"Sheriff!" Arnie Coleman shouted, "this has been goin' on too long. You gotta let us in there."

"Nobody goes inside, unless you're willin' to do it without a gun."

"That ain't right!" somebody yelled.

"And if you do go in, you can't interrupt the town council meetin'."

"Ain't no meetin' goin' on in there," Coleman said. "Just a damned poker game."

"Well, take off your gun, Arnie, and go in there and tell them that."

"I ain't takin' my gun off while the Gunsmith's around," Coleman said. "He killed Big Ed."

"You can't prove that, Arnie."

"What if I told you I could?" Coleman asked. "What then?"

"What? You got proof?"

"What would ya need as proof?" Coleman asked.

"Well," the sheriff said, "it would help if somebody had actually seen Adams around the ranch."

"Okay, I got men out lookin' for Ray Gomez. He was at the ranch this mornin', and maybe he seen somethin'."

"Well," Yatesman said, "if he did, then bring him to me and let him tell me."

"And then what?"

"And then I'll go inside and arrest Adams."

"We don't want him arrested," somebody shouted, "we just want you to bring him out."

"Yeah," somebody else yelled, "we'll take care of him ourselves."

"You boys just sit tight," Yatesman said. "Let's hear what Gomez has to say and then we'll figure out what to do."

"So," Clint asked, "they're just sitting around out there waiting for this Gomez to show up?"

"That's about the size of it."

"Well, where is he?"

"Seems he took some time off, so they're out lookin' for him."

"Well then," Clint said, "I guess we better wait to hear what he has to say before we start worrying. Lawson, you wanna deal those cards?"

ELEVEN

"I don't think I ever asked you, Adams," Mayor Patton said. "What brought you to Cannon City in the first place?"

"Curiosity."

"Curiosity?" Lawson asked. "About our town? What the hell for?"

"Cannons."

"What?" Chambers asked.

"I thought it was full of cannons," Clint said. "Otherwise, why the name?"

"It was supposed to be called Canyon City," the judge said. "That's what we all agreed on."

"And what happened?" Clint asked.

They all looked around and then the judge said, "Somebody spelled it wrong on the charter."

"And we became Cannon City," Patton said.

"Well, wait a minute," Clint said.

"What?" the judge asked.

"There isn't a canyon here, either," Clint said.

* * *

Since the game was going to go on all night the saloon remained open while others in town closed. That meant that anyone who wanted a drink was now in there. Also, rather than running from the possible confrontation that was brewing, people were gathering inside the saloon, and outside, to see it. The town council meeting had suddenly developed a circus atmosphere.

The sheriff came walking into give the judge a report on what was going on.

"So far the deputies have succeeded in holding back the ranch hands."

"Nobody wants to risk getting shot, right?" the judge asked. "No one wants to be the first one through the door."

"I told them they can come in, but they have to leave their guns outside," Yatesman said. "Nobody is willing to do that."

"Well," Ben Lawson asked, "if the deputies are holdin' them back, what've you been doin', Sheriff?"

"I've been out there, too, Lawson," Yatesman said. "I know you been wanting to replace me, but I've been doin' my job."

"If I may say so, Sheriff," Clint said, "it doesn't sound like you have."

"Whaddaya mean?" the sheriff demanded.

"Well, what have you done to find out who shot Ed Kennedy?"

"I've been tryin' to keep you alive," the lawman said, "that's what I've been doin'. If you woulda let me put you in my jail, I could've been doin' somethin'.

"Yeah," Clint said, "somethin' to prove I was guilty, so when the Bar K men killed me in your jail you wouldn't be responsible."

"So what do you think I should be doin', huh?" Yatesman demanded.

"If I was you, I would have gone out to question the other two ranchers by now," Clint said.

"I haven't had the chance!"

"That's bullshit, Sheriff," the judge said. "You been sittin' on your hands, waitin' for this Gomez feller to show up and prove that Clint Adams killed Ed Kennedy. What happens when he can't do that? You'll have to start from scratch."

The judge looked at Lawson.

"You know, Ben," he said, "I'm startin' to think you may be right. Maybe we do need a new sheriff."

"Judge—"

"Get out there and prove me wrong, then, Pete," the judge said. "Find out who killed Big Ed Kennedy; don't just go along with the mob that wants to lynch Clint Adams for it."

"I don't think they'd bother with a rope, Judge," Clint said. "It sounds like they just want to put me up against a wall and execute me—firing-squad style."

"Not while I'm the judge in this county," the judge said.

"Judge—"

"No more excuses, Sheriff," the judge said. "Get out there and start your investigation."

"I ain't a goddamned detective!" Yatesman snapped.

"Maybe not," the judge said, "but you're the closest thing we've got, right now."

Yatesman looked around the table and found no supporters. He turned on his heel and stormed out.

"He's right, you know," Chambers said. "He's not a detective."

"And we don't have the time to call a real detective in," the judge said. "We've got to go with what we've got."

"Well, I don't," the mayor said, throwing in his hand, "not with these cards. I fold."

TWELVE

At first light the sound of a buckboard could be heard entering town, along with the sound of horses. The sheriff, his deputies, and the Bar K men in the street all turned their heads to have a look. Finally, the buckboard came into sight, with riders flanking it.

"Great," one of the deputies said. "That's Matt Holmes from the Double H."

"This saves me the trouble of havin' to ride out and talk to him," the sheriff said.

"Might save us a lot of trouble if this bunch and that bunch would kill each other," the deputy said.

"Yeah," Yatesman said, "that would clear the way for Andy Rivers and the Triple R ranch to take over, completely."

As they watched the buckboard stopped. The riders fanned out on both sides of it. A man stepped down and faced the saloon and the men in the street.

"Sheriff?" Matt Holmes shouted.

"Here," Yatesman said.

"Am I safe to approach?"

"Leave your men where they are," Yatesman said. "I guarantee your safety." He looked at Coleman and the Bar K men. "I'll kill the first man who fires a shot. Arnie?"

"Yeah?"

"If I can't identify the man who fired first, I'll kill you. Understand?"

"I understand," Coleman said. "Let's hear what the old buzzard has to say."

"Come ahead, Mr. Holmes," Yatesman said.

As Matt Holmes drove his buckboard into town he quickly sized up the situation. Apparently, the word he'd gotten was correct. Clint Adams was inside the saloon. What he still didn't know was whether or not it was true that he was playing poker with the judge, the mayor and a majority of the town council.

Once he got the sheriff's assurance of safety he turned and spoke to his foreman.

"Lee," he said, "anyone fires a shot, you and the boys know what to do."

"Yes, sir," Lee Jackson said.

"Okay."

Matt Holmes started walking forward.

Sheriff Yatesman did not step down into the street to meet Holmes. He remained on the boardwalk in front of the saloon with his three deputies. Matt Holmes had to walk in among the Bar K hands. He stopped directly in front of the sheriff.

"I heard Ed Kennedy was dead. Is that true?"

"It is."

"Killed by the Gunsmith? Clint Adams?"

"We're still tryin' to figure that out."

"Adams killed him, all right," Coleman said. "And he's inside, being protected by the judge and the mayor."

"Is that true?" Holmes asked, without acknowledging the presence of Arnie Coleman.

"It's true that Adams is inside," Yatesman said. "But we still don't know for sure that he killed Kennedy."

"I see," Holmes said.

"What are you doin' here, Mr. Holmes?" the sheriff asked.

"I knew that if Ed Kennedy was dead, murdered, you'd have two suspects," the older man said. "Me and Andy Rivers. Well, I'm here to tell you that I had nothing to do with Ed Kennedy's death."

"You could've hired Clint Adams to do it," Sheriff Yatesman said. "Or somebody who was impersonating Clint Adams."

"If I wanted Ed Kennedy dead, I'd kill him myself," Holmes said.

"Then maybe Rivers had it done."

"Andy Rivers would no more hire a killer than I would," Holmes said.

"Are you sure of that?"

"Dead sure," Holmes said. "If I know Andy, he's on his way here right now."

"With some of his men?"

"No doubt," Holmes said. "Your town is about to become an even bigger powder keg, Sheriff."

"So what do you want, Mr. Holmes?" Yatesman asked, still with respect.

Matt Holmes pointed past Sheriff Yatesman, at the saloon.

"I want to go inside."

"Why?"

"I want to talk to Clint Adams," Holmes said.

"What for?"

"I'll tell him."

Yatesman stared at Holmes for a few moments, then said, "I'll have to check."

"You do that."

THIRTEEN

Sheriff Yatesman appeared at the judge's side while the man was laying down a flush.

"You win," Clint said, tossing his hand onto the table.

"Ha!" the judge said, raking in the pot, "I told you the tide would change. Only took what, about thirty-six hours or so? Forty?"

"Who's countin'," Ben Lawson said.

"You're still way behind, Judge," the mayor said.

"Not as far behind as you are," the judge said happily.

"Don't remind me."

"Don't you fellas want to take a break?" Clint asked. "Aren't you tired?"

"Forget it," Chambers said. "Just keep dealin'. What else have we got to do?"

"Don't you folks have day-to-day business to conduct?" Clint asked.

"This is what we do day in, day out," the mayor explained. "This town stopped growing a long time ago, and it pretty much operates itself."

"Judge?" the sheriff said.

The judge looked up at him.

"Sheriff," he said, "when did you come in?"

"A few minutes ago," Yatesman said. "I'm sorry to interrupt your, uh, meeting, sir, but Matt Holmes is outside."

"What's he want?" the judge asked.

"He wants to come in."

"What for?"

"To talk to Adams."

Clint looked at the judge.

"Who is he?"

"One of the other ranchers," the judge said. He asked Yatesman, "Is he alone?"

"No, he's got a bunch of his boys with him, and he thinks that Andy Rivers is probably on his way to town with some of his boys."

"Ka-boom," Lawson said. "That'll be like lighting a match to a powder keg."

"That's kinda what he said."

"Well," the judge said to Clint, "what do you think?"

"Sure," Clint said, "let him in. Let's see what the man has to say."

Yatesman went out and came back in with Matt Holmes. Others in the saloon—some of whom had been dozing after being there all night—perked up, thinking that maybe the action was about to start.

"Mr. Holmes," the judge greeted.

"Judge. Since I recognize everyone else at the table, I assume you must be Clint Adams?"

"That's right," Clint said.

"You're the man who is supposed to have killed Ed Kennedy."

"And you're one of the men who possibly paid me to do it."

"I'm Matthew Holmes," the white-haired man said. "I own the Double H."

"What can I do for you, Mr. Holmes?" Clint asked.

"I want to offer you sanctuary."

"What?"

"I will take you to my ranch right now," Holmes said, "and guarantee you safe passage out of town."

"Now why would you want to do that, sir?"

"Because I don't like seeing anyone get railroaded for something they didn't do."

"What makes you think I didn't do it?"

"Well, I didn't hire you," Holmes said, "and I doubt that Andy Rivers hired you. And if you were being hired by Kennedy to kill us, why would you kill him? You see, none of this makes any sense to me."

"Well, sir, I appreciate the offer of sanctuary, but I can't accept."

"I have enough men outside to get you out of town," Homes assured him.

"I'm sure you do, but if I took you up on this, Mr. Holmes, then everyone would be convinced that you hired me to kill Big Ed Kennedy. You see? It wouldn't do either one of us much good."

Holmes took a moment to think, then said, "I see you're an intelligent man, sir. That makes me all the more certain that you did not kill Kennedy, so despite all that you say being true, my offer stands."

"And I still appreciate it," Clint said, "but no, thank you, Mr. Holmes. I believe I'll take my chances right here."

"But, by staying here you're endangering all these people." Holmes swept his arm around to indicate the saloon full of men.

"These people are free to leave whenever they want,"

Clint said. "They're here because they don't want to miss a bloodletting. They deserve whatever they get."

"Again," Holmes said, "I can see we're in agreement. Very well."

"Will you and your men be leavin' town, Matt?" the judge asked.

"It would probably be better for all if we got out before Andy Rivers get here," Holmes said. "Sir, may I shake your hand?"

Clint looked up at Holmes, then stood up.

"If you don't mind doing it left-handed," Clint said, extending his left hand and keeping his gun hand free.

Holmes chuckled, said, "Sir," and shook hands with Clint left-handed. The he looked at the members of the town council. "Gentlemen."

"Thanks for comin' in, Matt," the judge said. "Probably saved us a bunch of bother."

"Don't mention it, Judge."

"Sheriff?" the judge asked. "You got any questions for Mr. Holmes before he leaves?"

"No, sir," the lawman said, "I'm convinced he didn't have nothin' to do with killin' Ed Kennedy."

"Then have a good day, Matt," the judge said. "I got to get back to my meetin'."

FOURTEEN

When the sheriff and Matt Holmes got outside, both groups of men were ready to shoot it out. Both foremen were in the middle of the street with their jaws jutting out and their gun hands ready.

"Coleman!" Yatesman shouted. "Don't you pull that hogleg out."

"Lee!" Holmes shouted. "Get the men turned around. We're leaving."

Both men turned and looked at Yatesman and Holmes and then backed off.

"Good-bye, Sheriff," Holmes said. "I wish you luck—and don't believe Andy Rivers as easily as you believed me."

"About . . . hiring Adams?"

"Yes," Holmes said. "Andy is devious. He just might have done it."

"But . . . do you think Adams killed him?"

"No," Holmes said, "but I wouldn't put it past Andy Rivers to hire an imposter. So . . . good luck."

"Thanks."

Matt Holmes stepped into the street, grabbed his foreman's arm, and walked over to his buckboard. He climbed aboard—assisted by Lee Jackson. The foreman then mounted up, turned his men around, and headed out of town. Matt Holmes turned his buckboard and followed.

"What happened inside?" Arnie Coleman demanded.

"Nothin' much," the sheriff said. "Matt Holmes is convinced that Clint Adams didn't kill your boss."

"He's coverin' for him!" Coleman said. "Can't you see that?"

"There's no proof," Yatesman said.

"So what are you gonna do?"

"Well, I was gonna ride out to talk to Andy Rivers, but Mr. Holmes figures Mr. Rivers is on his way here, so I'm gonna wait. If he doesn't ride in soon, I'll go and see him."

"What for?"

"To ask him if he hired Clint Adams," the sheriff said. "What about your guy, Gomez?"

"We still ain't found him."

"Well, keep your men in line, Arnie," Sheriff Yatesman said.

"Sooner or later," Coleman said, "somebody's gonna get brave."

"Gettin' brave is the same as gettin' stupid," the lawman said. "Is it gonna be you?"

"You never can tell, Sheriff," Coleman said. "You just never can tell."

Inside the judge looked at Clint between hands and asked, "What do you think?"

"About what?"

"Matt Holmes," the judge said. "Why would he make an offer like that?"

"He obviously doesn't think I killed Kennedy."

"Or he's coverin' for you," Lawson said.

"Leave it to a lawyer to come up with that conclusion," Clint said.

"I'll bet it's the same conclusion they're comin' to outside."

"Then why are you here, Lawson?" Clint asked. "You obviously think they'll be coming in for me sooner or later. Lead's going to be flying soon."

Lawson smiled.

"We told you," he said. "This is all we do. I'm ready for a little excitement."

Clint looked around the saloon and said, "Apparently, so is the whole town.

FIFTEEN

It took a couple of hours but eventually they heard the sound of a buggy and many horses.

Yatesman was surprised they could hear it. The street was usually crowded with activity at this time of the morning, but the entire town seemed to be on hold since this business had started. And as long as Clint Adams was in the saloon with the town council, everybody would be waiting for something to happen.

When the buggy came into view Yatesman could see Andy Rivers driving it. Behind him came a handful of his men with his foreman, Parker Stark.

Rivers stopped his buggy just about where Matt Holmes had stopped his buckboard. He was a smaller, lighter man than Holmes, just a few years younger. There was more spring in his step as he approached the sheriff. His foreman remained behind, standing with his legs spread. As far as Yatesman was concerned, Stark was more gunman than foreman, but the lawman had never had any cause to go against him.

"Sheriff."

"Mr. Rivers."

"I saw Matt Holmes on the road," Rivers said. "Seems he and I had the same idea."

"Which is?"

"To come to town and tell you that I had nothing to do with Ed Kennedy's death."

"I see."

Rivers looked around.

"Looks like you have a big job on your hands," Rivers said.

"I'm handlin' it."

"Good for you," Rivers said. "Where's the judge?"

"Inside," Yatesman said. "There's a . . . meetin' goin' on."

"Yes, I heard something about that."

"I suppose you wanna go inside?"

"That sounds like a good idea," Rivers said. "Just to . . . pay my respects to the judge."

"I'll have to go in and check."

"You do that, Sheriff," Rivers said. "I'd appreciate it."

"Now what?" the judge asked when the sheriff appeared at his elbow. He was not happy, having just lost a hand with a full house to Clint's larger full house.

"It's Andy Rivers, Judge," Yatesman said. "He wants to come in."

"And I suppose he's out there with that foreman of his and a bunch of men?"

"Yeah, he is."

"That foreman?" Clint asked.

"Name of Stark," the judge said. "Parker Stark. Gunman, if you ask me."

Clint frowned.

"Seems I've heard that name before," he said.

"Maybe you have," thc judge said. He looked at Yatesman. "What's he want?"

"Said he wants to come in and pay his respects to you."

"To the judge?" Mayor Patton asked. "Not to the mayor?"

"All he said was to the judge."

"Oh, all right," the judge said. "Let him come in, but alone. Tell 'im to leave that snake outside."

"Yes, sir."

Yatesman walked Andy Rivers into the saloon. The man wore a pearl-handled revolver on his right hip. Clint watched him walk and knew he wore the gun for show. That was why he had a man like Parker Stark as his foreman.

Clint recognized Stark's name. The man had a reputation in Texas as a hand with a gun. That was about ten years ago. Since then no one had heard anything from him. Apparently, he changed careers from gunman to ramrod.

Of course, a ramrod who could handle a gun was of great value to a man like Rivers.

Clint was surprised when the judge stood up to greet Rivers. He didn't know if this was in deference to the man, or the man's right hand—Stark.

"Nice to see you, Andy," the judge said, shaking hands.

"Judge." Rivers look at Clint. "This the fellow who is supposed to have killed Ed Kennedy?"

"Andy Rivers, this is Clint Adams."

"The Gunsmith," River said. "Did you kill Kennedy, son?"

Clint looked at Rivers and asked, "Did you hire me to do it?"

"I did not."

"But you wouldn't need to hire anybody," Clint said. "You've already got somebody in your employ who could do it."

"You're talking about Stark," Rivers said. "He's a good man, but he didn't do it."

"How do you know?"

"Because he only does what I tell him," Rivers said, "and I did not tell him to kill Ed Kennedy."

"Well," Clint said, "nobody told me, or asked me, or hired me to do it, and I had no reason to do it on my own because I never met the man."

"Andy," Judge said, "I hope your men aren't gonna start any trouble outside."

"Not likely, Judge," Rivers said. He switched his gaze from Clint to the judge. "That is, unless I tell them to. As long as Kennedy's men behave themselves, I won't have to do that."

"Did you run into Matthew Holmes on the road, Mr. Rivers?"

"I did."

"Did he tell you about the offer he made me?"

"He did."

"And you two didn't come to blows?" Clint asked. "Your men weren't tempted to draw down on each other?"

"If I have a man in my employ who will draw his gun without first being told by me, I would fire him."

"So," Clint asked, "how often did you and Mr. Holmes work together against Ed Kennedy?"

Rivers glanced around the table, then at the judge, but when he looked at Clint his glance turned into a stare.

"What makes you think Matt Holmes and I have ever worked together?"

Clint smiled.

"I just don't think you and your men could encounter him and his men on the road without somebody ending up eating some dirt—unless . . ."

"Nice seeing you, Judge," Andy Rivers said. He turned and walked out of the saloon.

The judge sat down, looked around the table.

"Well," he said.

"You know," Patton said, "it makes sense. Those two always seemed to be one up on Big Ed."

"If that was the case," Clint asked, "then why was it necessary to kill him?"

SIXTEEN

The question hung over the table.

"That's true," Ben Lawson said. "If they were teaming up against him, there was no need for either one to want him dead."

"So, the question is," Clint said, "who else had a reason to want him dead?"

Again, the town council exchanged glances.

"How about you gents?"

The cards remained on the table as *that* question hung over them.

"That's ridiculous," the judge said. "Why would anybody at this table want to kill Ed Kennedy?"

"That's what I've been saying," Clint pointed out. "But at least you fellas knew him. I didn't."

"Ed Kennedy was very important to this town," the mayor said. "So are Matt Holmes and Andy Rivers. The three of them keep this town alive with their business."

"Doesn't mean somebody from this town didn't want him dead," Clint said. "I happened to walk in here as the big, bad stranger and I'm getting the blame. It's easy to point a finger at the stranger in town, isn't it?"

The judge drummed his fingers on the tabletop.

"I don't like the direction this is takin'," he said.

"Once it's proven that I didn't kill him, people are going to start looking elsewhere."

The cards stayed on the table.

"Still want to play poker?" Clint asked.

"You know," Lawson said, "Yatesman is never gonna be able to figure this out."

"We need somebody who can," Chambers said.

Now all four men looked at Clint.

"Not me," he said. "I'm a suspect, remember?"

"I think if you did it, you'd've been gone a long time ago," the judge said. "Since we have a quorum, here, I say we vote on whether or not to hire Adams to solve the mystery of Ed Kennedy's death."

"All in favor," the mayor said, and the four men all said, "Aye," at the same time.

"Nay," Clint said.

"Sorry," the judge said, "you ain't a member of the council."

"But I'm the guy you're trying to hire," Clint said. "Why should I help a town that's so ready to string me up for something I didn't do?"

"It ain't the town that's ready to string you up," the judge said, "it's the Bar K boys."

"And they're still out there," Clint pointed out. "To take you up on your offer I'd have to be able to get out of this saloon."

"You could slip out the back," Lawson said.

"Somebody would tell them as soon as I did."

"We can make sure they don't," Chambers said.

"How?"

"We'll empty the saloon," the judge said. "We'll say the meeting's too important and we need to have the saloon to ourselves. Once everybody's out, you can slip out the back."

"And walk around town?"

"How many of the people in town do you think would recognize you walking the streets?" the mayor asked. "Hell, I ain't sure they even recognize me when I'm on the street."

Clint looked around the table. All four men were staring at him.

"What about the game?" he asked.

"We'll keep the game goin'," the judge said, "but I think we all need some rest. Why don't we take a break to empty the saloon, catch a nap, and then work on getting Adams out the back door?"

"Wait a second," Clint said. "I haven't agreed to anything, yet."

"Yet?" the mayor asked.

"He means money," Lawson said.

"Well," Clint said, "the word you used was 'hire.' "

The other three glared at the judge.

"Well, you can't expect him to do it for nothin'," the judge said. "Why would he?"

"Ain't he got enough of our money over the past two days?" Chambers asked.

"Consider that as payment for poker lessons," Clint said. "Wanting me to solve a murder . . . that's extra."

"Okay, how much?" the judge asked.

"I don't know," Clint said. "I'm still not sure I want to do it."

"Well," the judge said, "just because we believe you didn't do it doesn't mean anyone else does."

"But if you tell people . . ." Clint said.

"And why should we?" Lawson asked.

"And who says we all believe you didn't do it?" Chambers asked.

Clint looked at the judge, who just shrugged.

"That's blackmail," he said.

"Could be called that," the judge said, "but blackmail wouldn't involve payment, so why don't we just agree that you'll be paid and discuss a price?"

"You drive a hard bargain, Judge," Clint said.

SEVENTEEN

The game broke up briefly, which meant the town council meeting was in "recess."

Clint found Jennifer and asked her if he could use her room.

"Should I come up with you?"

"After a while," he said. "They're going to start emptying the saloon. Come up when that's done, so you can let me know."

"And how long will we have?" she asked.

"Long enough for me to take a nap and make some decisions," he said.

"Ooh," she said, "a nap sounds like fun."

"Waking up from a nap can be fun," he said, "if you get my meaning."

She smiled.

"Nobody ever said I was slow," she told him. "Okay, the door's open. Go ahead. I'll be up there in a little while."

Clint didn't know where the council members went to get their rest. And he didn't know how much luck they were having downstairs emptying the saloon. He walked to the window and looked out. It was dark again and the Bar K men were once again carrying torches. He wondered how long it would be before somebody got the big idea to toss one through a window.

He was surprised that Sheriff Yatesman and his temporary deputies seemed to be doing the job, keeping the Bar K boys out of the saloon. Now, as he watched, people started to come streaming out of the saloon. He wondered what the reaction would be on the street.

He decided to actually try to get some sleep before Jennifer showed up. Also, he had some thinking to do about the killing of Ed Kennedy. He and the town council had come to an agreement on price, and he was now charged with solving a murder—and solving it would ultimately prove that he was not the one who killed the man. The money was secondary.

He removed his boots and lay down on the bed, fully dressed, with his gun hung on the bedpost. He had decided, after all these years, that bedposts had been invented for him to hang his gun on.

He clasped his hands behind his head and wondered what his detective friends like Talbot Roper and Heck Thomas would do?

When Sheriff Yatesman saw everyone leaving the saloon he thought it was all over. Had Adams slipped out the back and made his escape, after all? He wanted to go in and find out, but he had to wait for everyone to come out, first.

When the Bar K foreman, Arnie Coleman, saw the men filing out of the saloon he wondered what the hell was going on.

"Hey, Arnie," one of the other men asked, "what the hell—"

"I know, I know," Coleman said. "Keep your eyes open, men. Adams might be tryin' to slip out with the crowd."

"And if we see 'im?"

Coleman turned to his men and said, "If anybody has a shot at Adams, take it!"

EIGHTEEN

Yates finally made his way into the saloon and caught the bartender and owner by the arm.

"What's goin' on, Sammy?"

"I dunno," Sammy said. "The judge tol' me to empty the saloon, so I'm emptyin' the saloon."

"Why?"

"I dunno," Sammy said, again. "Ask 'im. You know, I was doin' a heckuva business. Now I'm supposed to close? By the time I open again all these men will go back to their regular saloon."

Sammy walked away, shaking his head.

Yatesman looked for the judge, spotted him at the back of the room with the mayor, and hurried over to the two men.

"Judge, Mayor, is it over?"

"Nothin's over, Sheriff," the judge said, "we just wanted to empty the saloon."

"Why?"

"We want the rest of our town council meeting to be private," the mayor said. "That's all you gotta know."

"Sheriff, your job is still to keep the Bar K boys at bay."

"Keep 'em where?"

"Out of the saloon," the mayor said, "just like you been doin'."

"But—"

"Don't ask any questions, Pete," the judge said, slapping the lawman on the back. "Just keep doin' your job. You've been doin' great."

"Wha—really? Well, okay . . ."

Now the judge's slap turned into a push toward the door.

"Just keep doin' your job," he said, again.

As the sheriff went back out the doors Sammy closed and locked them, then turned to stare at the judge and the mayor.

"Don't worry, Sammy," the judge said. "It's temporary."

"You got some empty rooms upstairs?" the mayor asked.

"Sure," Sammy said. "The girls went up to their rooms, but there's a couple. I think Mr. Chambers and Mr. Lawson took one. You and the judge can have the other one."

"What say, Mayor?" the judge asked. "Roommates?"

"Just for tonight, Judge. Sammy, we'll be back down to continue our meetin'."

"What am I supposed to do until then?" the saloon owner asked.

"We're takin' a short rest, Sammy," the mayor said. "I suggest you do the same."

"Yeah," Sammy said, "rest."

Clint woke up with Jennifer tugging at his trousers. He'd taken his boots off, so once she got his belt undone the trousers gave in to her insistent tugging.

"Jennifer—"

"Quiet," she said, "just lie there and rest."

Was she taking his pants off to make him more comfortable—or to make herself more comfortable?

It became clear once his pants were off and she went for his underwear, running her hands over his bare thighs.

"Jenn—"

"I'm gonna relax you," she told him, sliding his underwear off.

His cock had already gotten the message and was getting harder and longer.

Now he noticed she had turned the flame on the wall lamp up when she entered. He had turned it down before he fell asleep.

She stepped back and reached behind herself to undo her dress, slide it down her shoulders, and step out of it. She had no undergarments on. He didn't know if this was always the case, or if she had started doing that since his arrival. He didn't mind, though. Her full breasts came into view, and as she massaged them the nipples became harder, and so did he.

Naked, she joined him on the bed, and this time she rubbed her big breasts over the bare skin of his thighs. She did that for a little while, kissing his belly at the same time, and then eventually took his rigid shaft between her big breasts and rolled it there. The head of his dick peeked up from her cleavage, and she ran her tongue over it.

"Relax me, huh?" he asked. "I'm not feeling very relaxed at the moment."

"I'm not, either," she said, grinning up at him, "but don't worry, we both will be . . . soon."

When the front doors of the saloon were locked Arnie Coleman said aloud, "What the hell is goin' on?"

He ran forward, but stopped short when the sheriff and his deputies turned to face him.

"What's goin' on, Sheriff? Where's Adams?"

"He's inside, as far as I know, Coleman."

"As far as you know?" Coleman demanded. "How do we know he didn't slip out the back?"

"Because I have a man in the back to make sure none of you slip in," Yatesman said, "and I'm sure you have a man to make sure he doesn't slip out. And neither of us has heard anythin'."

"Why are they lockin' the saloon up?"

"I told you, the meetin' is gonna be private."

"What're they doin' now?"

"Takin' a break," Yatesman said. "They'll start up again, soon."

"And what're we supposed to do?"

"How about you all go home?" Yatesman asked.

"Not while the man who killed our boss is still in there," Coleman said, pointing at the saloon.

"Well then, I guess we're all just gonna have to keep waitin' out here, like we been doin', ain't we?"

NINETEEN

By the time Jennifer slid the entire length of Clint's cock down her throat he was ready to explode. She kept it there for a few seconds, then slid him out again. She smiled as she took hold of him at the base and squeezed, taking his urge away. She knew what she was doing, this girl.

"I'm not gonna let you finish until I use you up," she told him. "Do you mind?"

"Like you said," he told her, "I'm just going to lie here."

"Good."

She slid up his body until she was lying directly on top of him, her big breasts and his huge erection both crushed between them. She kissed him, a hungry, searching kiss, tongue avidly plunging into his mouth. Then she sat up on him, took hold of his penis, lifted her hips, and slowly slid him inside of her.

"Oh!" she said, and he grunted as her insides gripped him.

Coleman pulled Charlie Hicks over to the side, into the shadows where the others couldn't see him.

"Charlie," he said, "you're gonna be the one to kill Clint Adams."

"By myself?" Hicks's eyes popped open.

"You're our best rifle shot," Coleman said. "I want you to get up on the roof and wait for your chance."

"When?"

"Now," Coleman said, "go up there now. Find a good spot. Nobody will be able to see you in the dark."

"But, Arnie . . . is this the right thing to do?" Hicks asked.

"Charlie, if I offered this chance to any of the other men, they'd jump at it. Adams killed our boss, and you're gonna be the one who makes him pay."

"I—I don't know if I can do it, Arnie."

"Who wins the turkey shoot every year?"

"I do."

"Ain't nobody can shoot a rifle like you can, kid," Coleman said. "You get up there and you wait for your chance. I know you can do it."

"Okay, Arnie," the pumped-up young man said, "okay, I'll do it!"

Jennifer's bobbing breasts had Clint's eyes mesmerized. He watched as the nipples danced before his eyes, and when he couldn't just watch anymore he reached for her and took hold. He squeezed them tightly, enjoying how solid they felt in his hands, how heavy they were, how hard the nipples were.

Jennifer was in a world of her own. All she was aware of was how his penis felt inside of her. She rode him up and down, then stopped to grind herself down on him and swivel her hips, growling deep in her throat at the same time.

Clint forgot that there were twenty men or more waiting outside to kill him. The sounds she made, the feel of her, the smell of her, that was all he was aware of in that room. Sex with Jennifer was all encompassing. She fucked with such abandon that he gave her the attention he deserved.

And the good thing about her, the absolute best thing, was that she knew they were having sex and not making love.

Women like that were rare.

TWENTY

This time when Jennifer woke Clint it was just to get him up.

"You said you wanted me to wake you up."

He looked at her, saw that she was dressed, looked down at himself, and saw that he was still naked.

"You better get up and get dressed before I get back into bed with you," she said. "Then you won't get out of this room for hours."

"Thanks for the warning," he said. "Jennifer, while I get dressed would you look out the window and tell me what you see."

"Sure."

She walked to the window and looked out.

"I see a lot of men holding torches," she said. She turned and looked at him with concern. "They're not gonna burn the place, are they?"

"I doubt it," he said. "I don't think they'd sacrifice everybody in this building just to get me. They figure I've got to come out some time."

He finished dressing, then took his gun from the bedpost and strapped it on.

"You're not gonna go walkin' right out there, are you?" she asked. "Even you're not good enough to outdraw twenty men, are you?"

"I don't think so," he admitted. "I think fifteen would be my limit."

"No, really . . ."

"No, really," he said. "I'm not going out there—at least, I'm not going out the front door."

"You wanna go out the back?"

"I think that would be best, don't you?"

"Well, yes . . . would you be coming back?"

"I hope to get out and back before they even know I'm gone."

"I could help."

"How?"

"Well, I think you know that I could be a . . . distraction if I want to be."

She was grinning at him, and he smiled right back at her.

"You know," he said, "I think you might just be helpful, at that."

When Clint came downstairs with Jennifer, the judge and the mayor were sitting at the "meeting" table. They were not playing cards, however. They were drinking coffee.

"Where are our other members?" Clint asked.

"Still asleep, we assume," the judge said.

"Maybe they're with the other girls," Jennifer suggested.

"Oh, I don't think so," the mayor said. "They have wives."

"And they're old," the judge said. "As old as us, anyway."

Jennifer laughed. "Neither one of those things means they ain't with one of the girls."

The judge and the mayor looked at each other. Maybe Clint thought, they were thinking they could have been with one of the girls.

"What are you plannin' to do?" the judge asked Clint, getting away from the other subject.

"Are you gonna take us up on our offer?" the mayor asked.

"I am," Clint said.

"So what are you gonna do?" the judge asked.

"I'm going out the back," Clint said. "And, hopefully, I'll be able to come back that way, as well."

"How do you propose to get out?" the mayor asked.

"Jennifer's going to help me with that," Clint said.

"Why bring her into this?" the judge asked.

"Because she offered," Clint said.

"What can she do?" the mayor asked.

Jennifer, who had been wearing a shawl around her shoulders, now removed it. Underneath she had on a dress that revealed her creamy shoulders and much of her big breasts. She took a deep breath, which made her breasts swell even more. Both the judge and the mayor had to moisten their mouths and swallow.

"She's going to distract whoever's watching the back," Clint said.

"Uh," the mayor said, "I think you're right."

"Yeah," the judge said, "I don't think she'll have much trouble distracting whoever's back there."

"But how will you get back in when you come back?" the mayor asked.

"That," Clint said, "I'm going to have to figure out for myself."

TWENTY-ONE

Sheriff Yatesman had been wrong.

The Bar K boys did not have someone around the back of the saloon. Arnie Coleman didn't think that Clint Adams was the kind of man to slip out the back. If a man with a reputation did that, his entire reputation would change. It just never occurred to the foreman.

So when Jennifer went out the back door there was only one man there. Ollie Park was one of Yatesman's temporary deputies. He was a young man who thought that wearing a badge would be exciting. When Jennifer came out the back door with her shawl worn low, he found something even more exciting.

Her breasts.

"Well, hello, deputy," Jennifer said.

"M-miss."

Jennifer could see this was going to be even easier than she'd thought. The young man could not take his eyes off her partially exposed breasts.

She walked up to him, then walked around him, getting him to turn his back to the rear door of the saloon. Clint stuck his head out, took a quick look, and then slipped out the door and into the shadows.

Jennifer talked to the young deputy for another ten minutes before going back inside.

Clint made his way through the shadows to the livery stable. The big front doors were locked, but he found a side door that he was able to force with no trouble.

"Hey, big boy," Clint said, finding Eclipse's stall. "How you doing?"

Eclipse moved around impatiently.

"You want to run, don't you?" Clint asked. "Yeah, me, too." He patted the horse's big neck. "Yeah, well, you're going to get to run, but I'm not."

Clint saddled the big Darley Arabian, wondering what would happen if he rode out of town and just kept going. No, he'd have to do more than that. He'd have to keep going . . . and going . . . and going . . . and change his name. If the word got out that the Gunsmith had cut and run, young guns would be looking for him all over the West.

There was not chance of that. Clint was tired enough after all these years of carrying his reputation. He didn't need to give gunmen more reason to seek him out.

Once he had Eclipse saddled he had to get the large doors open as quietly as possible. He decided he only needed to open one door—which he did—and then walked Eclipse out and closed the door behind them. He mounted up and rode Eclipse slowly and quietly out of town.

Chambers and Lawson came down from upstairs and joined the judge and the mayor at the table.

"What were you fellas doin'?" the mayor asked.

"I was asleep," Chambers said.

"So was I," Lawson said. "Why, what did you think we were doin'?"

"Never mind," the judge said, picking up the cards. "Let's get back to business."

"Speakin' of which," Ben Lawson said, "where's our Mr. Adams?"

"He decided to take us up on our offer," the mayor said. "So he's out there . . . somewhere."

"He'll be back," the judge said.

"Not if he decides to keep goin'," Lawson said.

"And not if those Bar K boys find him," Chambers said.

The judge dealt out the cards and said, "He'll be back."

TWENTY-TWO

Clint didn't know where he was going.

If he was going to look into the murder of Big Ed Kennedy, he thought the place to start was the Bar K ranch. Only he didn't know where the Bar K was. It was dark, too dark to try to track his way there—and even if it wasn't dark, which tracks would he follow? The Bar K men had ridden in, so had the Double H boys and the Triple R hands. That would leave a lot of tracks.

But as is often the case, fate takes a hand in men's lives, and it did today.

Clint heard the light tinkling of a bell up ahead of him. In the moonlight he saw a drummer's wagon coming toward him. The bell was obviously somewhere on that wagon.

Clint was sitting still on Eclipse and he decided to remain that way. If he rode up to the drummer, he might frighten him, might make him think he was being robbed. So he just sat and let the man reach him on his own.

The drummer did, indeed, see him and reined his horse in.

"Hello, friend." The man driving the wagon was middle-aged, scruffy-looking. Clint didn't know what he was selling, but he didn't think he'd ever buy anything from him.

"Howdy," Clint said.

"Heading for Cannon City?" the drummer asked.

"Actually," Clint said, "I just came from there."

"A little late to be traveling, isn't it?"

"I thought I'd be able to find my way in the dark," Clint said. "As it turns out, I got turned around."

"Where were you headed? I spend a lot of time in this area and can find my way pretty well in the dark."

That was good news to Clint.

"I was trying to find the Bar K ranch."

"Big Ed's place?"

Clint nodded, wondering if the drummer had heard about the rancher's murder.

"Hell, that's the easiest place to find," the man said. "I can give you good directions."

"Well," Clint said, "I'd be much obliged if you could get me there."

"No problem," the drummer said. "Ya see, you go north about . . ."

Clint followed the drummer's directions and rode right to the Bar K ranch with no problem. He also rode his horse up to the house without being challenged. Apparently, everyone from the ranch was in town. But just to be on the safe side he rode around back and left Eclipse there.

He found a way in through the back—going in and out back doors was getting to be a habit—and found his way to the rancher's office, where the man had been found dead behind his desk.

As he entered the room he saw the blood on the desk

and on the floor. He got behind the desk and avoided the blood as best he could while giving the desk a thorough search. Then he looked around the office, trying to find anything in the dead man's files that would help him figure out who he had actually hired while he was thinking he had hired Clint Adams.

"Are you a burglar?" a woman's voice asked.

Clint looked up quickly. A middle-aged woman was standing in the doorway, holding a glass with a brown liquid in it. She looked to be about forty-five, but she was a handsome woman, apparently a wealthy rancher's wife who had taken good care of herself.

"Mrs. Kennedy?" Clint asked.

"That's right."

"I'm sorry," he said. "I thought everybody had gone to town."

"Everybody who wants revenge on the man who killed my husband did," she said.

He stood straight up.

"And you don't want revenge?"

She sipped her drink, then said, "No."

"Why not?"

"Because he stopped bein' my husband a long time ago," she said.

"There were . . . difficulties between you?"

"You said it."

She had a lot of red hair, and it fell to her shoulders in waves. She was wearing a robe, Clint assumed over a nightgown. But she didn't look as if he had awakened her—unless she had taken to sleeping with a drink in her hand.

"If you don't mind me asking . . . what kind?"

"What kind didn't we have?" she asked, laughing. "For

one thing we had separate bedrooms. He hasn't touched me in years."

"Well . . . I'm going to assume by looking at you that your husband was much older than you."

"Not 'much' older," she said, "but you're sweet. Yes, he was older, but he had his other women—younger women—so he really hasn't been a husband to me . . . oh, I don't know. But it's been years."

"How long have you been married?"

"About twelve years," she said. "I was no spring chicken when he brought me here, but I soon learned he hadn't brought me here for sex. He just wanted someone who would look good—respectable—on his arm."

"And have you—were you respectable?"

"Are you asking me if I had other men?" she asked, making her eyes wide. He noticed they were a very pretty green.

"Well—"

"No, that's okay," she said. "You can ask me. The answer is no, I did not have other men." Then she frowned. "Or is the answer yes, I have been respectable?"

"I think it's pretty much the same either way, ma'am," he said.

"Oh, don't call me 'ma'am,'" she said. "At least I know I'm not considerably older than you are."

"No, ma—uh—"

"My name is Barbara."

"That's a lovely name."

She took another sip of her drink.

"No one's said anything that nice to me in years," she said. "You know, my husband was such a powerful man around here that men were afraid to talk to me, let alone sleep with me."

"I'm sorry."

"So am I," she said. "I've become a dried-up old prune."

"If I may so say, Barbara, you don't look dried up, at all."

She studied him for a moment, her pretty lips pursed, then asked, "Would you like to come and sit with me and have a drink?"

"Well—"

"There's no one else on the whole ranch," she assured him. "No one."

"All right," he said.

"Come with me."

She led him out of the room.

TWENTY-THREE

He followed her swaying ass down the hallway. There was certainly nothing dried up about her. She looked as if her full-bodied figure had been very well preserved.

She took him into a sitting room and said, "Have a seat anywhere. I'm having whiskey. It's my husband's—late husband's—very best."

"That sounds fine," he said.

She poured him a drink, then topped off her own glass. She carried both drinks to the sofa he had seated himself on, sat next to him, and handed him one. He noticed she had given him the glass with the least liquid.

"What's your name?" she asked.

This would be a good test.

"Clint Adams."

"I'm happy to meet you, Clint Adams," she said, clinking glasses with him.

He sipped the whiskey. It was, indeed, very good stuff.

"What can I do for you, Mr. Adams? Are you here to steal? Investigate? What?"

"Investigate, I suppose," Clint said. "The town council has hired me to look into your husband's murder."

"That's because they know the sheriff is incapable of finding out who killed him."

"Barbara, who do you think killed him?"

"I don't have any idea," she said. "You probably thought I had a lover who did it, but I didn't have a lover. Haven't had a lover for a very . . . very long time. Don't you think that's a shame, Clint?"

"Yes," he said, "I think it's a terrible shame."

He noticed that, somehow, while she was pouring drinks, she had managed to undo her robe and open it, revealing a very nice pair of breasts encased in a silk nightgown. The slopes of her breasts, and her cleavage, were dotted with freckles.

"But you didn't tell me, Barbara," Clint said, aware that there was heat coming from her body, "who do you think killed your husband?"

"Well," she said, "I think the first person who should be suspected is . . . me. After me, I suppose Matt Holmes and Andy Rivers would seem likely."

"Did you know that Holmes and Rivers would sometimes work together against your husband?"

"No," she said, "but I'm not surprised. Those two were here before Big Ed got here. And I suppose him coming here gave them a common enemy. So they stopped fighting with each other to fight against him?"

"I suppose so."

"They hid it well, then," she said, "because everybody in town still thinks of those two as competitors."

"Well, maybe they only joined forces when it involved your husband."

"That could be true," she said, "but then why kill him?"

"That's what I was thinking."

"Well then, I see your point, Mr. Adams," she said. "I guess that just leaves me."

"I don't think you killed him."

"Well, maybe I had him killed."

"By who? You already told me you didn't have any lovers."

"What if I hired it done?"

"Would you know how?"

"Oh my, what's to know?" she asked. "You find a man and you offer him money. If you offer him enough money, he'll do it."

"You think it's that simple?"

"When you have enough money," she said. "What if I offered you, say, a thousand dollars to kill my husband? What would you say?"

"I'd say let me see the money," Clint answered. "Do you have that much money to spend, Barbara?"

"No," she said, "but I'd have it after my husband was dead."

"And you think a man would kill your husband for an IOU that he can collect on after the job is done?" he asked.

"Well," she said, "I'm ashamed to say that I know for a fact that they won't."

"You mean you tried?"

"Yes."

"And you got no takers?"

"None," she said.

"And should I believe you?"

"Oh my," she said, "after we've been so frank with one another, why would I lie about a thing like that? I tried to have my husband killed, no one would do it, but someone finally did."

"And has anyone come forward for the money?"

She blinked.

"Oh, I see," she said, "you think I just put the amount out there and asked for takers? No, no, I talked to several men directly. This was not a . . . what would you call it? An open offer."

"So someone else killed your husband, for reasons having nothing to do with you?"

"That's how I see it," she said. "No lovers, no hired guns. Another drink?"

TWENTY-FOUR

Arnie Coleman knew he was doing the right thing. He just wished he had somebody more reliable than Charlie Hicks. The kid was a crack shot with a rifle, but he was young. Coleman didn't think he'd killed anyone before. He just hoped that wouldn't stop him from taking the shot when he had it.

Charlie Hicks was scared.

He knew what Arnie Coleman told him was true. Clint Adams deserved to die for killing Big Ed Kennedy. And Charlie was the best shot on the ranch. He knew both of those things were true, but the other truth he knew was that he'd never shot anything but an animal before and that was only when he was hunting for food.

He got up on the highest roof he could find and hoped that when the time came he'd be able to take the shot. If he didn't, he didn't see how he could stay on the ranch anymore.

* * *

"I know who you are, you know," Barbara Kennedy said to Clint.

"What?"

She nodded.

"The hands were talking, and Arnie Coleman told me that you killed Ed."

"Did he tell you why?"

"No."

"Or how he knew?"

"He said everyone knew Big Ed was going to hire you," she said.

"To do what?"

"Nobody knows," she said. "Arnie thought it might be to kill Andy Rivers or Matt Holmes."

"Did your husband ever say anything to you about having them killed?"

"Oh no," she said, "Big Ed never talked to me about his business."

"Did he ever talk to anyone about his business?" Clint asked.

"I assume Arnie, since he's the foreman."

"So Arnie *would* know if Big Ed had hired me," Clint said. "And he'd know why."

"I guess."

"And he'd know if Big Ed *didn't* hire me."

She sipped her drink and noticed her glass was empty.

"I would say so. Could you fill my glass for me again, please?"

"Sure."

He stood up and she handed him her drink. From that position he was looking right down the front of her nightgown.

"So," he continued, yanking his eyes away from her cleavage and walking across the room, "Arnie Coleman should be the only man who knows the whole truth."

"If you say so. Are you coming with that drink?"

He poured some whiskey in the glass and carried it back to her. She reached for the glass and took it. Her other hand brushed against his thigh as he sat back down next to her.

"Barbara, would Arnie Coleman have any reason to kill Big Ed?"

"I don't think so," she said. "I mean . . . why would Arnie kill the man who was paying him?"

"Maybe," Clint said, "Arnie got fired?"

"I don't know anything about Arnie getting fired," she said.

"You said your husband didn't talk to you about his business," Clint said. "So why would he tell you if he had decided to fire Arnie?"

She tapped her nail on the glass she held.

"So Arnie is trying to blame you?"

"By telling all the hands that Big Ed was hiring the Gunsmith," Clint said. "That's why they all knew about Big Ed's plans. And for everyone to know, that would be unusual, right?"

"Yes, correct," she said. "Tell me, how do you intend to prove this?"

"Well," he said, "we'll have to question all the hands, find out how they heard that Big Ed was planning to hire me."

"And?"

"And I'll need you to testify that your husband would only discuss his business with his foreman."

"So, you need me to come to town with you?"

"Yes."

"Tonight?"

"Well . . . that would be helpful."

She thought it over for a few moments, then said, "I don't think so."

TWENTY-FIVE

"What?"

"I don't want to ride into town tonight."

"But . . . why not?"

"Well . . . for one thing," she said, "I'm kind of drunk. Who's going to believe anything I say in this condition?"

Clint had been wondering when she would show some effect of the whiskey she was drinking. He assumed she'd been drinking before he got there, and so far she was remarkably lucid.

"I think I can convince the judge to believe what you say, Barbara."

"Well, maybe, but . . . I still don't want to go."

"Why not?"

"You need me to do this, don't you?"

"Yes, of course," he said. "I wouldn't ask you if I didn't need you."

"Well," she said, "I need you, and I need you to do something for me, first."

"Okay."

"And after you do something for me," she said, "then I'll do something for you."

"Okay, Barbara," he asked, "what do you want me to do for you?"

She put her drink down, settled her hands primly into her lap, tossed back her hair, and looked at him.

"I want you to fuck me."

"Barbara—"

"Now, hear me out," she said, raising one hand. "I know that's a rather lowbrow word for what I want you to do, but that's what I want. I don't want to 'make love,' and I don't want to 'have sex.' What I want to do, pure and simple, is fuck."

"Barbara, I don't have time—"

"Where do you have to go?" she asked. "Back to town? To take sanctuary in the saloon again? I have a wonderful bed upstairs. All you have to do is come up there with me, get naked with me, sweaty, and fuck."

"Is that really what you want?"

"Oh, yes," she said, reaching out and running her hand over his thigh. "Yes, yes, yes, Mr. Gunsmith. I told you, my husband hasn't touched me for years, and no other man dared while he was alive. I need to find out if what you said earlier is right."

"What did I say earlier?"

"That my juices are not all dried up." She leaned forward and gripped his thigh tightly. Her breasts almost fell out of her nightgown. "Do you know why I dress like this to go to bed?"

He had to moisten his mouth to answer.

"No, why?"

"Because I like to touch myself when I'm in bed," she

said. "No, that's not right. It's because I have to touch myself, because nobody else will."

"Barbara—"

"I need a man's touch, Clint Adams."

"You have a lot of men working on this ranch," he said. "I'm sure any one of them would be happy to oblige you."

"You're probably right," she said, "and now that Big Ed is dead I'll probably pick out a couple, but tonight . . . I want you."

She stood up, looked down at him, and dropped her robe to the floor.

"I'll make it easy for you," she said.

Next, she shrugged off the nightgown.

"I'll let you see what you'll get if you agree."

She had a marvelous body. Full breasts and hips, brown nipples, nice thighs, only the slightest signs that she was in middle age. And her smell—she was in heat, all right, like an animal, and he could smell her—and like any male animal, his body reacted.

She reached out and took his chin in her hand.

"Stand up and kiss me," she said. "If you tell me you didn't like it, I'll get dressed and go with you."

So that was his way out. All he had to do was kiss her and tell her he didn't like it. How hard could that be?

He stood up and faced her. The heat coming from her body actually made him start to sweat. But he was in control. He knew he could do this. A simple kiss, and then they'd be on their way.

But two things undid his resolve as he leaned forward and their lips met. It wasn't that she pressed her body against him, crushing her breasts into his chest.

And it wasn't that the smell of her started to make him dizzy.

It was something she did and a sound she made.

First, just before their lips touched she moistened her mouth with her tongue. It was an incredibly sexy thing for her to do at that moment.

And second, as their lips met, she made a sound into his mouth. He wasn't sure he could describe it, because it was a decidedly female sound.

The only way he could describe it was that it was kind of like . . . "Mmmm."

TWENTY-SIX

"Where do you suppose he went?" Delbert Chambers asked the table at large.

"Maybe he went to see Rivers and Holmes," Ben Lawson suggested.

"Why would he do that?" The judge asked. "Both of them came here and spoke to him."

"Maybe he wants to see each of them alone," Lawson said.

"Yeah," Chambers said, "maybe he wants to beat the truth out of them."

"Or threaten them with his gun," Lawson said.

"Didn't the two of you pay any attention when he was here?" the judge asked. "That's not the kind of man he is."

"The judge is right," the mayor said. "Adams wouldn't threaten them with his gun—he'd just shoot them."

Lawson looked at the mayor.

"You think he killed Kennedy?"

"No," the mayor said, "I don't."

"You know," the judge said, "you can ask him all these questions when he comes back."

"You really think he's comin' back?" Lawson asked.

"Oh yes," the judge said, "I'm certain of it."

"How certain?" Lawson asked.

All four men put their cards down.

"Are you proposing a wager, Ben?"

"This is interesting," Chambers said.

"Quiet," the mayor said. "Let's listen to Ben and the judge."

"I say Adams is gone," Lawson said, "never to return to this table, this saloon, or this town."

"And how much are you willin' to risk on your belief, Ben?"

"Two hundred?"

"You don't have much faith in your beliefs, do you?" the judge asked.

"Okay, five hundred," Lawson said. "Five hundred dollars says Adams doesn't come back."

"I'll cover that, Ben," the judge said, "but I've got another five hundred that says he's back by this time tomorrow."

"What time is it, Delbert?" Lawson asked.

Chambers took out his watch and checked the face.

"It's ten p.m."

"All right," Ben Lawson said, "five hundred more says he's not back by this time tomorrow."

"We'll each write two checks," the judge said, "and the mayor will hold them."

"Agreed," Lawson said.

"Well, get to writing the checks, then," the mayor said, "so we can get back to our game."

TWENTY-SEVEN

Andy Rivers sat in the most comfortable chair in his study and smoked his cigar. On the table next to the chair was a snifter of brandy. When Parker Stark came to the door he stopped right there.

"Cigar?" Rivers asked.

"No."

"Brandy?"

"No."

Rivers took his cigar out of his mouth and blew a long plume of smoke before speaking again.

"Every time you come in here I offer you a cigar and a brandy, and you always say no. Why is that?"

"You pay me for my services, Mr. Rivers," Stark said, "and you pay me well. I wouldn't enjoy your cigars and your brandy. I smoke three-for-a-nickel cheroots and drink rotgut . . . and I like it. You wanted to see me?"

"Yes," Rivers said. "Do you think you can take the Gunsmith?"

"I don't know," Stark said. "How can anybody know that?"

"I'd like you to try."

"Then the question is," Stark said, "can you pay me enough to try?"

"I might have a bottle of cheap whiskey around here somewhere, Stark," Rivers said. "Maybe we can have a drink and . . . discuss it?"

"Why not?"

Over drinks—Rivers expensive brandy, and Stark cheap rotgut whiskey—they discussed the price and came to an arrangement.

"When do you want it done?" Stark asked.

"Tomorrow."

Stark finished his whiskey and stood up.

"I want it done in the street, Stark," Rivers said, "All legal."

Stark sat down, poured the last of the rotgut into his glass.

"We have more talkin' to do."

By the time he finished that glass they had agreed on a price. Stark would face the Gunsmith in the street and kill him. Hopefully.

Stark stood up.

"Half now, half after it's done," Rivers said.

Stark sat down.

"Give me some of that brandy you're always braggin' about."

By the time they finished their brandy Stark saw the wisdom of Rivers's offer.

"If he kills me," he said, "I won't have any need of the second half."

"Or the first, for that matter," Rivers said.

"I might be able to figure out a way to hedge my bet," Stark said. "Any objection to that?"

"As long as it looks legal," Rivers said, "I don't have a problem."

Stark stood up, staggered a bit.

"That brandy of yours has quite a kick," he said.

Or, Rivers thought as Stark went out the door, half a bottle of rotgut.

TWENTY-EIGHT

Clint kissed Barbara Kennedy, and then kept on kissing her. While he was kissing her, and feeling her body against his, he thought, well, why not? What was the rush to get back to town? The morning would do.

His hands roamed over her body, kneading her opulent flesh, enjoying the feel of her smooth, hot skin.

Her hands were between them, doing some kneading of her own through his pants.

Finally, the kiss broke and she pulled her head back, but did not take a step back.

"So?" she asked. "What's the verdict?"

"Can't you tell?"

She squeezed him through his pants.

"Yes, I think I can."

She took his hand, then led him to the stairway, up to the second floor, along a long hallway to her bedroom. Inside he saw the bed she had been talking about. It was, as she had said, wonderful—large, comfortable, perfect for sex or sleep . . . or both.

She pulled him to the bed, then kissed him again, long

and hungrily. He could taste the whiskey on her, but combined with her own sweet taste it was not unpleasant.

He broke the kiss and stepped back to look at her again. She was breathing hard, her breasts heaving, and her nipples were standing out irresistibly.

"Your husband has been a fool for many years," he said. "In fact, any man who wouldn't want you would be a fool."

"Oh, for chrissake," she said, "stop talking!"

He smiled at her and began to take off his clothes. She pulled the bedcovers down and got in bed to await him. Reclining on the bed she was even more exciting to look at.

He crawled onto the bed and onto her. This was a body that deserved time, and they had all night . . .

Matt Holmes stood at the front window of his house and gazed out at his ranch—or what he could see of it in the moonlight. His wife of forty years came up behind him, handed him a cup of tea.

"What are you thinking about?" she asked.

"Ed Kennedy," he said. "The West is going to miss him. We needed men like him."

"You hated Ed Kennedy," she said.

"Yes, but I admired him, too. I certainly would never have hired anyone to kill him."

"So who do you think hired this man . . . the Gunsmith . . . to kill him?"

"No one."

"Then why did he do it?"

"I don't think he did."

She sipped her own tea and said gently, "All right, then, who did? Andy Rivers? He has that gunman, Stark, working for him."

"Andy's more likely to send Stark after Adams. He wouldn't have sent him after Kennedy."

"You're sure of that?"

"Very sure."

"Well then," she said, "I suppose the killer came from Kennedy's own ranch."

He looked at his wife. His eyes always saw her as they had first seen her, forty-one years ago—a vibrant, lovely young woman. As soon as he laid eyes on her he knew they would marry.

"You're a very smart woman," he said.

"Smart enough to say yes to you when you asked me to marry you."

"Happiest day of my life," he said, touching his wife's face.

"So, tell me," she said, "do you intend to get involved in all this Ed Kennedy hoopla?"

"No, not involved," he said. "I'll just remain an interested observer."

"And you won't let Andy Rivers draw you into anything?"

"No," he said, "I'm still my own man, Martha."

"I haven't forgotten that, Matthew," she said.

They stood for a few moments in front of the window, he with his arm around her waist, and she with her head on his shoulder.

After a while she said, "I'm tired. I'm going to bed. Are you coming?"

"In a few minutes," he said. "I think I'll sleep better if I have one more brandy."

"Well, you know what drinking does to you," she said. "Don't expect me to wake up all eager to pleasure you."

"You pleasure me every single day we're together, Martha," he assured her, kissing her lightly on the lips. "Go to sleep and sweet dreams. I won't wake you when I come to bed. I promise."

TWENTY-NINE

Clint wanted to take his time with Barbara, but she was insistent. She grabbed at him, his erect penis, and tugged him on top of her.

"Put it in, put it in!" she demanded. "You can be gentle later. I just want you to pound me!"

Well, he thought, okay, if that was what she wanted. He certainly had some frustrations he could work out by "pounding" her.

He got on his knees between her legs, pressed the head of his penis against her wet pussy, and . . . rammed himself in.

That was what she wanted. Her eyes went wide and she breathed, "Oh yeah! Finally!"

She wrapped her legs around his waist.

"Yeah, yeah, come on, do it . . ." she said, as he started to pound away at her.

He grabbed her legs, pulled them away from him, took her by the ankles, and spread her wide. Holding her that way, he gave her what she wanted and took what he wanted.

It was a win-win situation.

* * *

Parker Stark went back to the bunkhouse to turn in for the night. Finally, he'd made the deal that would set him up for life somewhere. Working for Andy Rivers, squirreling away his paycheck, trying to save the money he'd need to get settle somewhere was taking a long time. But now, with one act, he could make enough money to change his life.

All he had to do was live long enough to enjoy it.

Stark had a corner of the bunkhouse to himself. There were more bunks than men, and since he didn't really interact with the other men, they all made sure their bunks were away from his.

The other men in the bunkhouse were afraid of him. That always suited him. But in his new life, he was going to be someone else. One way or another, facing Clint Adams in the street was going to be the last act of Parker Stark's life.

He'd either succeed and walk away, leaving "Stark" as dead in the street as Clint Adams.

Or he'd be the one lying in the street dead, all alone.

True to her word Barbara let Clint go slow next time, but he didn't expect that the next time would be right away. They were both so out of breath after the first time that he was surprised when she came right back at him.

"No rest," she said, flipping him on his back with surprising strength. "I don't know when my next time will be, but I'm almost certain that it won't be with you. So come on." She grabbed his penis. "Get hard again."

"It doesn't work that way, Barbara," he complained. "You can't just say 'get hard.' There's got to be some rest involved."

"I'll show you rest," she said. "Just lie back."

She stroked his penis with one hand while using her other hand on other parts of his body. Before long he was hard again. She sucked him wetly, stroked him, fondled his testicles, and then smiled up at him and said, "Oh, you don't need any rest."

She crawled up on top of him and sat down on him, taking him inside.

"Oooh, I'm gonna go real slow, this time."

He grabbed her hips and said, "That's fine with me."

The town council had learned one thing from Clint Adams as a group.

Take a break.

The judge and the mayor went to the bar. They didn't know where Chambers and Lawson went. Probably upstairs to get some sleep.

"For a bunch of old men we sure are puttin' in a lot of hours," the mayor said.

"I can never sleep, anyway," the judge said. "Might as well play poker."

"You know," the mayor said, "I can't sleep, either. Drives my wife crazy, me prowling around the house all night."

"I know how you feel," the judge said. "Funny, we've known each other for years, and we didn't know this about each other."

"I wonder what else we don't know?"

They got a beer each from Sammy, who was still fuming over being closed.

"When do I get to open up again, Judge?" he asked, setting them up with beers.

"As soon as Clint Adams gets back, Sammy."

"Great," the bartender said. "Are you payin' for these?"

"Put it on my tab."

"Figures."

As the bartender stormed off the mayor asked the judge, "You really believe Adams is comin' back?"

"I wouldn't have risked five hundred dollars if I didn't," the judge said.

"Five hundred. The bet I heard was a thousand?"

The judge laughed.

"I figured you'd be good for the other half. We are partners, right?"

"Have been for forty years," the mayor said, "but this time I would like to have been asked."

"You don't think he's comin' back?"

"I think we might have backed a killer and let him get away, all to get a poker lesson."

"It was more than that, Walter," the judge said. "We were bored, lookin' for somethin' to lift the boredom, and in walked Clint Adams."

The mayor stared at the judge, sipped his beer, then started laughing.

"It is the only excitement we've had for quite a while, isn't it?" he asked.

"It is."

"What will you do if Adams ends up in your courtroom?" the mayor asked.

"I'll do what I always do," the judge said. "Listen to the evidence and make an impartial judgment."

"You could make an impartial judgment on Clint Adams in this instance?" the mayor asked.

"I can," the judge said, and then added, "that is, unless he costs me five hundred dollars."

THIRTY

Barbara rode Clint slowly. Rather than sliding up and down on him, she was grinding her hips, moving them back and forth, forward and back and round and round. She kept her eyes closed, a dreamy look on her face, making noises deep in her throat, like the sound she made when he first kissed her.

Clint found it fascinating to watch her. He fondled her breasts, kissed her nipples, massaged the flesh of her thighs, feeling the muscles beneath. She was the quietest woman he'd ever been with. He'd heard women moan, groan, cry out, yell, and scream during sex. This one seemed to be keeping all of that inside, and he didn't know how.

Finally she began to ride him up and down, slowly at first, then faster and faster as she began to chase her orgasm. And even then, even when she was overwhelmed by the sensations, even when the cords one her neck stood out and the muscles in her thighs became as hard as iron, she remained silent . . . until she collapsed on him with a great sigh.

* * *

"I'd like to ask you something."

"Hmm?" She was lying on his shoulder, her hand making circles on his belly.

"How can you be so quiet during sex?" he asked. "I mean, after going without it for so long, I'd think you'd be . . ."

"Screaming?"

"Well, yes."

She laughed.

"Not very modest, are you?" she asked. "I'll bet you've made a lot of women scream in your time. You know, I could've been having sex with my husband for years, I still never would've had a night like you've given me tonight . . . so far."

"So far?"

"We're far from done," she said. "You still have a chance; you might make me scream, yet."

Clint thought he could have spent the whole night on Barbara's breasts and nipples. Her breasts were as heavy and firm as Jennifer's, even though Jennifer was much younger. And Barbara's nipples were so big when they swelled that he loved just rolling them in his mouth. They were like gumdrops.

She was still quiet while he sucked and licked her nipples, making those sounds deep in her throat. He squeezed her breasts then, making her catch her breath, squeezed them and bit them and sucked them . . . and then kissed his way down her body until his face was nestled between her thighs. She was very wet and he lapped it up, spreading her pussy lips so he could run his tongue up and down, and also in and out. He felt her breathing quicken, until she was almost gasping, and suddenly it became his goal to make her cry out. Not necessarily scream, but at least make some sound.

"Ooh, ooh," she said, reaching down for his head. She tried to push him away. "I know w-what you're trying to d-do, you bastard!" she said.

He didn't answer. That would have meant taking his mouth off of her, and then he would have had to start again.

No, he didn't move his mouth, but he also brought his fingers into play. While he licked her, wetting her even more, he slid first one finger inside of her, and then a second. He slid them in and out as his tongue circled her hard little clit. He had learned all he could over the years about a woman's body. He had even talked to doctors about them. He loved women and absolutely loved giving them pleasure. And he knew that was why women liked him. He knew what to do.

He kept working on Barbara's pussy, and at one point slid his hands beneath her ass, cupping her and lifting her so he could really press his face into her. He used his lips, and his tongue, even his teeth and, once or twice, his nose. She was gasping and writhing beneath him and finally, as her body went as taut as a bow, it finally happened.

"Oooh, ahhhh," she cried out, "ohh, yessss . . . damn you . . . all right . . . you win . . ."

She went over the edge, tumbling into her orgasm with abandon. She bucked and shook and quivered and tried to push him away but he persisted, kept going and going until, finally . . .

She screamed.

"God," she said, moments later, "Jesus, God, were you . . . trying to kill me?"

They were lying side by side, naked, and she kept running her hands over her own body, as if she couldn't believe what he had done to her.

"Hey," he said, reminding her, "this was your idea, not mine."

"I know," she said, "I know . . . it was a good idea, wasn't it?"

"Oh, I thought you were complaining."

"Me?" she asked. "I've got nothing to complain about. You were everything I wanted, and much more."

They lay there for a few moments, each catching their breath.

Then she said, "Do you want to know why I was so quiet? Why it was so hard for me to . . . let go?"

"Why?"

"Because for years," she said, "the only pleasure I got was from . . . myself. Here, in my bed. With my own hands. So I had to be quiet. I couldn't let . . . him . . . hear me."

"I understand."

"But now, tonight, there's nobody in the house," she said. "Nobody but me and you."

"And you let go."

"Finally," she said. "It was wonderful just to . . . scream."

"And it was loud."

She laughed.

"Sorry," she said. "I'll try not to be so loud, next time."

"Next time?" he asked.

"Well, yes," she said, turning on her side to look at him. "You didn't think we were done, did you?"

"Well, I thought . . . the way you say I was all you had wanted . . . I thought that meant we'd at least . . . get some sleep?"

"Well," she said, "I did mean that, when I said it. But

what I really meant was that . . . you gave me all I wanted . . . so far."

"So far?"

She smiled.

"Take a little nap, darling," she said, running her finger from his forehead to his chin, and then sliding her finger into his mouth.

"But just a little one," she said, "because we're not finished . . . yet."

THIRTY-ONE

It was an amazing night, but finally, a few hours before dawn, they both fell asleep. When they woke up and she started to crawl onto him with her big, naked, hot body, he slipped out from beneath her, falling onto the floor.

"What are you doing on the floor?" she asked, looking down at him with an amused smile.

"Oh no," he said, "we're done. I'm not going to let you get me started again."

"I could do that?" she asked. "Get you started again?"

"Yes, you could," he said, "very easily, and then we'd never get to town."

"Oh," she said, "town. I haven't been to town for a long time."

"Well, it's time for you to keep your part of the deal, Barbara. Remember?"

"Yes," she said, "yes, I do remember."

"So, get up, get dressed, and let's get going."

"Without a bath?" she asked, appalled.

"A bath?"

"Yes," she said, "and frankly, you could use one, too."

A bath didn't sound like a bad idea. After all, they did both kind of . . . smell, after their exertions all night.

"Okay," he said, "okay, a bath. But a quick one. I want to get going."

"Well," she said, "I know how we can bathe quicker," she said.

"How?"

"You draw the water for me . . ." she said.

"I could do that."

". . . And then we'll take a bath . . . together."

"Together?" He got up off the floor, grabbed his pants, and hopped on one foot and then the other as he pulled them on. "Oh no. I'll draw you a bath, madam, but we're not getting into the tub together."

She pouted. "Why not?"

"Because," he said, hurrying to the door, "we'd never get out again."

He went out, then a few seconds later he opened the door and stuck his head in.

"Where *is* the bathtub?"

Eclipse was pissed, and Clint didn't blame the animal. He'd been left out front, saddled, all night. Clint felt bad. While Barbara bathed he took Eclipse into the barn, unsaddled him, rubbed him down, fed him, and didn't dare tell the horse he'd be saddling him again in about a half an hour.

He went back inside, and while Barbara dressed he took a quick bath, using the same water, and kept the door locked so she couldn't sneak in with him.

The last thing he'd expected, the night before, when he had sneaked into the house, was the kind of night he'd spent with the not-so-grieving widow. He hoped that whatever ranch hand she chose as her next lover would be able to keep up with her.

Or the next two.

The woman had enough sexual energy built up that she could probably keep several ranch hands busy trying to satisfy her.

He had taken his clothes and his gun into the bathroom with him, so that when he came out he was fully dressed and had his gun strapped on.

He went to Barbara's bedroom to see if she was ready. When he didn't find her there he went downstairs. Maybe she was in the kitchen getting something to eat.

She wasn't in the kitchen.

He checked the rest of the house, but after the kitchen he knew.

She was gone.

THIRTY-TWO

Clint got to the barn and saddled Eclipse. He looked around, but he hadn't noticed earlier how many other horses were in the barn. He looked around, saw the tracks on the ground. Could have been any of the horses the hands had ridden into town, but then he saw the small boot marks—her boot marks. She'd quickly saddled a horse, led it out, walked it about a hundred yards from the house and barn, then mounted up and rode.

He had two choices. He could follow her trail, track her, see where she was going, or he could go back to town and work on his theory about Arnie Coleman, the foreman. Maybe he could convince the judge without Barbara that Coleman had a motive, since he was the only one who knew his boss's business.

And maybe Barbara had lied to him. If she knew her husband's plans, then she could have told somebody else. And that would mean that Coleman wasn't the only one who knew.

Suddenly, Barbara was a bigger suspect than Coleman,

otherwise why run? And who or where was she running to?

Clint mounted Eclipse and started tracking.

Parker Stark saw a rider coming toward him. He reined in and waited, finally saw that it was Barbara Kennedy. He could tell because of her fiery red hair. She was riding hard and slowed when she spotted him. By the time she reached him he had dismounted. He reached for her horse, then went around to help her down. Immediately, they moved into a tight clinch, kissing.

"What's wrong?" he asked. "I was comin' to see you."

"No, no," she said, "it's Clint Adams. He's at the house."

"What's he doin' there?"

"I caught him in Ed's office, going through his things," she said.

"What was he lookin' for?"

"I don't know," she said. "Something that would clear him, I guess."

"What did you do?"

"I pretended I was drunk, pretended to pass out," she lied. "But he stayed all night, anyway. So this morning I sneaked out. I don't know when he'll notice.

"Pretty soon, I'll bet," Stark said. "Okay, this is what I want you to do. Keep riding. I don't know how good a tracker he is, but just in case he tracks you all the way, go to the Triple R."

"What do I do when I get there?"

"I don't know," he said. "Talk to Rivers for a while, about anything. He'll probably offer you coffee or tea or somethin'. Take it. Spend at least half an hour there."

"But he'll think—"

"That's right, he will."

"But . . . what if he's right behind me?"

"Don't worry," he said, "I'll slow him down."

"Are you going to kill him?"

"No," he said, "at least, not here." He didn't tell her about the deal he'd made with Rivers. He'd made that deal in case his deal with her didn't pan out. A man needed to cover his bases.

He helped her get mounted and said, "Don't stop again until you reach the Triple R."

"All right, darling," she said. "I'll do as you say."

He watched her ride away. She was an Eastern woman trapped in the West and eager to get out. She thought he was her way to get out, but she also thought he was going to go back East with her. What would a man like Parker Stark do in Philadelphia or New York? In the beginning all he'd wanted from her was her lusty body. Now all he wanted was some of her dead husband's money. With money he could have any lusty body he wanted—and younger.

He looked around for likely cover, first to hide his horse, then to secret himself while he waited with his rifle.

Barbara Kennedy's tracks were easy to follow. She was making no attempt to hide them. Apparently she didn't care if Clint knew where she was going. She probably just wanted to get there with plenty of time to do whatever she had to do.

He was crossing a dry wash when the first shot came. He launched himself from his saddle, grabbing for his rifle at the same time. He latched onto the weapon, and they both were flying to the ground as a second shot was fired. When he hit he rolled, held on to the rifle, and found cover behind a small boulder. It wasn't much, but just enough if he folded himself up.

Eclipse ran off to a safe distance and stopped. The horse did not panic when shots were fired. It had happened all too often.

He maintained his position and waited.

THIRTY-THREE

After a couple of more shots it became clear to him that somebody was keeping him pinned down while not seriously trying to hit him. He'd been right out in the open when the first shot came. At the very least it would have been easy to hit his horse.

Whoever it was, they were just trying to slow him down, give Barbara a chance to do what she had to do. She had an accomplice, and she had a goal. One person was trying to pin him down while she got to another.

Once he knew this he knew he had a good chance to get away. All he had to do was run for Eclipse, or get Eclipse to run to him, or meet the horse halfway. And hopefully, the marksman would not decide to put the horse down.

He gathered his legs beneath him, held tightly to his rifle and got ready. He whistled at the horse, who lifted his head and started for Clint at a gallop. Clint figured he had one shot at grabbing the saddle and swinging into it while the horse was still on the move. If he missed, he'd make too easy a target—one that might be too good to resist.

He took a deep breath and started running.

Eclipse came up on him quickly—almost too quickly. He heard the shots but ignored them. Somehow he managed to grab his saddle horn, swing himself into the saddle, and not lose his rifle. Once he was aboard he left the shooter behind. He rode back the way he had come for about a mile, then circled around, came back, and picked up Barbara's trail again. He was prepared for another attempt to bushwhack him—or delay him—but it never came.

Apparently, he'd been delayed enough.

Barbara Kennedy rode up to Andy Rivers's house, still unsure what she was going to say to him. Stark wanted her to kill at least half an hour with the man. She was going to have to do some quick thinking.

Rivers came out of the house himself to greet her, descending the stairs.

"Barbara, what a nice surprise," he said, taking hold of the horse's bridle. "To what do I owe this visit?"

"Actually," she said, "I just had to get out, Andrew, and I found myself in your neighborhood."

"Well, step down and we'll have some tea. How does that sound?"

She would have preferred a drink, but tea would take longer, kill the time Stark wanted her to kill.

"Thank you, Andrew," she said. "Tea sounds lovely."

He helped her down from her horse, taking the opportunity to put his hand on her ass. She hoped she wasn't going to have to have sex with him in order to stay in the house for half an hour.

She'd been introduced to Rivers by her husband, of course, and had seen him several times over the years of living with Big Ed, but they had never had any kind of in-depth conversation. Since he was a man—complete with a man's ego—maybe he'd think she was already looking for a replacement husband.

Rivers called one of his hands over.

"Take care of Mrs. Kennedy's horse," he said, handing the man the reins, "and see if you can locate Stark for me."

"Yes, sir."

"Come along, Barbara," he said, placing his hand on the small of her back, and then allowing it to slide a bit lower, "let's have that tea."

Clint followed Barbara Kennedy's tracks directly to another ranch. From his vantage point he couldn't tell whose ranch it was, but he was sure it had to belong to either Matt Holmes or Andy Rivers. He saw a metal arch over the gate that said Triple R, so he assumed that the ranch belonged to Rivers. He suddenly remembered that Holmes's ranch was called the Double H.

He sat his horse near a copse of trees, secure that he could not be seen from below. He watched as a man led a horse to the barn. He assumed it was the horse Barbara had ridden there.

What business did she have with Andy Rivers? Or was it even business? Could have been pleasure, but Rivers was well into his sixties. It had to be something other than a friendly meeting. Why would she be friendly with her husband's enemy? Had she helped Rivers kill her husband? Or perhaps used the man to get her husband killed? And if Rivers had wanted Kennedy dead, for any reason, he would have sent in Parker Stark.

So maybe Stark was the man to talk to now? Or Arnie Coleman?

Clint decided to wait and see how long Barbara spent in the Rivers house. Once she left he wouldn't follow her, though. It was about time for him to head back to town and the council meeting.

THIRTY-FOUR

"You know," Ben Lawson said to the judge, "even if Adams gets into town without bein' seen, he's got to get in the back door again. That's not gonna be easy with one of Yatesman's deputies out there."

The judge was standing at the bar with Lawson, having a beer.

"What do you care?" the judge asked. "That would just mean you win your bet."

Lawson looked over at the mayor and Chambers, who were involved in a hand that he and the judge had folded from.

"I don't care," Lawson said, "I'm just sayin'."

Lawson picked up his beer and walked back to the table with it.

The judge knew the lawyer was right. Clint Adams had to get back into the saloon by the back door—unless he tried to get in a window.

A window . . .

Now there was the germ of an idea.

* * *

The judge had Sammy bring Jennifer down, and he took her to the far end of the bar with him, so the other members of the town council could not hear them.

"You want me to do what?" she asked.

"Open a window in your room," he said.

"What if one of those creeps outside decides to come in?" she asked.

"Where is your window?"

"I have two. One looks out over the front street. The other one overlooks the alley."

"Can anybody get at the alley window? Is it hard?" he asked.

"No, there's a low roof outside of it. It's the roof of Sammy's storeroom."

"Okay," the judge said. "leave it open. I want Adams to be able to get in."

"Oh, I see," she said. "We don't know when he's comin' back so I don't know when to distract the deputy again."

"Right."

"And you have a bet goin' that he'll get back in."

"Right again."

"So," she asked, "how much is it worth to you for me to leave my window open?"

"Don't you want to help Adams?"

"Of course I do," she said, "but that doesn't mean I won't take advantage of a chance to make some money."

So they began to dicker.

Once Jennifer had her price she went up to her room and opened her window. She looked out and didn't see anyone. She knew the judge had a lot riding on Clint coming back, but she wasn't sure he would. With everything that was going on out front any sane man would just keep on riding.

Of course, given the reputation of Clint Adams, there was no guarantee he was sane.

Hell, she thought, there's no guarantee that any of us are sane.

The judge joined the others at the card table, picking up a hand that had been dealt to him. He'd had a hot hand since Clint Adams had gone. Apparently, he was the one who had learned the most from playing poker with Adams for so long.

"Whaddaya do, Judge?" Chambers asked.

"I raise," the judge said.

"Ya can't raise, ya damn fool," the mayor said. "Ain't nobody opened yet. It's up to you."

With a small smile the judge said, "Oh, sorry . . . I open."

THIRTY-FIVE

Clint walked Eclipse back into Cannon City. Even though it was daylight, there was nobody around the livery. The people were still inside, peering out their windows at what was going on near the saloon.

He unsaddled the big gelding, rubbed him down and fed him, then left the stable and use alleys to get back to the hotel.

He was able to see what was going on out front. The Bar K boys and the lawmen had been joined by others—mostly by some enterprising types who were taking the opportunity to make some money. With the saloon closed one of the other saloon owners had set up a temporary, portable bar and was selling whiskey and beer. He had also brought a couple of saloon girls out there with him.

The temporary bar had brought some of the men out of their homes and stores, and they were standing at the bar, drinking and waiting for the action to start at the smaller saloon.

On the boardwalk some people—men and women—had

gotten brave and had gathered to watch. One of the cafés in town had brought out some sandwiches to sell.

The whole thing had a very carnival atmosphere to it. All that was missing was the fat lady. Clint thought, at some point, he'd probably end up providing the trick-shooting entertainment.

He moved into the alley, wondering how he was going to get in the back door, when he spotted an open window on the second floor. It didn't take him long to figure out it was Jennifer's room.

He found a couple of barrels he could use to climb on so he could reach the lower roof beneath the window, then made his way to the open window, hoping this wasn't some kind of trap. He paused with one leg inside, wondering if Jennifer would be able to smell Barbara Kennedy on him. He shrugged, figured he had to take the chance.

He stepped inside.

The mayor took a hand.

The tide had turned again, away from the judge to the mayor.

Lawson sat back in his chair, rubbed his face, and said, "Got to be my turn sooner or later."

Sammy came over and said, "When will you guys get tired of playin' poker and go home? I need to reopen my place."

"Soon, Sammy," the judge said, "very soon."

Delbert Chambers was gathering up the cards for the next deal.

"Yeah, Sammy, as soon as the judge, here, admits that Clint Adams ain't comin' back you can open."

"Have you looked out the front window, Judge?" Sammy asked. "It's like a damn circus."

"Hmm? Oh, let me take a look."

The judge stood up and walked to the window. He looked out at what was going on and shook his head.

"I'm losin' business, Judge," Sammy said. "Look, they even got a bar out there."

Lawson laughed.

"Somebody put up a bar? Now that was good thinkin'," the lawyer said.

"Good thinkin'," the judge said, "but they got no permit for that."

"Hey, that's right," Sammy said. "Close 'em down, Judge!"

"I will, Sammy," the judge said. He walked back to the table. "As soon as Adams gets back."

"Why does my business depend on the Gunsmith?" the saloon owner complained. "He don't even live here in town."

"Don't worry, Sammy," Lawson said, "Adams will soon be takin' up residence in the jail."

"You think so?" the mayor asked. "I thought you bet the judge he wouldn't even be back."

"I'm hedgin' my bet," Lawson said, with a smile.

"I'll bet," the judge said, "that Clint Adams doesn't do a minute in jail. Any takers?"

"Not me," Lawson said.

"Why not?" the judge asked. "You're so cocksure of everythin'."

"Yeah, well," Lawson said, "you're the damn judge. You'll just make sure he don't go to jail."

"That would be dishonest of me," the judge said.

"Come on, Delbert," the mayor said, "deal out the cards."

"Don't forget me," another voice called.

They all looked over and saw a man coming down the stairs from the second floor.

"Deal me back in," Clint Adams said.

THIRTY-SIX

Clint took his first hand back.

"Sammy, bring me a beer," he called as he raked in the pot.

"I thought you didn't drink while you played?" Lawson asked. He was morose because he'd had to pay the judge a thousand dollars to square their bet.

"I've been exerting myself a bit since I left," Clint said. "In fact, I haven't had anything to eat."

"Come to think of it," the judge said, "neither have we. Joby!"

Nobody had seen Joby since the day before, but they knew the kid was always around. He came running out while Sammy set a beer at Clint's elbow.

"Joby, here's some money; go out front and get some sandwiches."

"Right, Judge!"

As the boy ran out the front door the judge said to Sammy, "You can leave the doors open if you like, Sammy."

"I can reopen?"

"You can reopen."

"Finally!"

Clint drank some beer and the judge said, "You gonna fill us in?"

"Yeah," Lawson said, "if you're back, you must have figured out who killed Big Ed Kennedy—that is, if you didn't."

"I've got an idea," Clint said, "but before I say anything I need to talk to someone."

"Who?" the judge asked.

"Arnie Coleman."

"What makes you think Coleman will talk to you?" the judge asked.

"Because you're going to tell him to," Clint said. "Have him sit in the corner and I'll join him."

"You don't want us to hear what you have to say?" Lawson asked.

"I really don't care," Clint said, "but Coleman might not want you to hear what he has to say."

"You sayin' Coleman killed his boss?" Chambers asked.

"I'm not saying anything . . . yet," Clint said. He looked at the judge. "Can you arrange that for me?"

"Sure."

"Right away?"

"How about after the sandwiches?" the judge asked. "And after we get some of our money back."

While they ate, the judge had Joby go out and fetch Sheriff Yatesman.

"Judge wants to see you, Sheriff," Joby said.

Yatesman turned and was surprised to see the front doors of the saloon open.

"Saloon open for business, Joby?"

"Yes, sir."

One of the deputies looked at the sheriff.

"Can we go in and get a drink, Sheriff?"

"No," Yatesman said. "Go in the back and change places with your brother."

"Yes, sir."

"Sheriff?" Joby said.

"Yeah, yeah," Yatesman said, "tell the judge I'll be right in."

"Yes, sir."

Yatesman waited, seeing Arnie Coleman come walking over.

"What's goin' on, Sheriff?" he demanded.

"The saloon's open again, Arnie," the sheriff said. "I'm goin' in to talk to the judge."

"What about?"

"I don't know," Yatesman said. "Guess I'll find out when I get inside."

"Well, tell the judge somethin' for me."

"What?"

"Tell 'im I don't know how long I can keep my men back," Coleman said. "They're gettin' pretty liquored up."

"I'll tell 'im," Yatesman said.

Yatesman had noticed that since the temporary bar had gone up his men were drinking heavily. All but the kid on the roof with the rifle. Yatesman figured he was there to take a shot at Adams first chance he got. He decided not to do anything about it, though. Just let nature take its course.

He turned and went inside.

* * *

"What's on your mind, Judge?" Yatesman asked.

"Sandwich, Sheriff?"

"No, thanks," Yatesman said. "I had some outside."

"I want you to bring Arnie Coleman in here," the judge said, "and sit him at that corner table."

"Am I supposed to ask 'im, or tell 'im?" Yatesman asked.

"You're supposed to bring him," the judge said.

"What's this for?"

"Don't worry about it, Sheriff," Lawson said. "Somebody else is gonna do your job for you. All you've got to do is bring him in.

"Now wait a minute—"

"Come on, Sheriff," the judge said. "Just do it."

Yatesman glared at Lawson, then looked over at Clint Adams.

"What?" Clint asked.

"Just surprised you're still here," the sheriff said. "That's all."

"What'd you think I did, slipped out the back past your deputies?"

"No chance."

Yatesman turned to go out, then stopped and looked at the judge.

"One more thing, Judge. Coleman says his men are getting all liquored up. He doesn't know how much longer he can hold them back."

"Okay, Sheriff. Thanks."

Yatesman left. Moments later he came back in with Arnie Coleman, who didn't seem to need to be forced. Coleman glared at Clint while Yatesman led him to the corner table.

"What's this about, Sheriff?" Coleman asked.

"You got me, Arnie," Yatesman said, "but you said you wanted in, so you're in."

The sheriff turned and walked out.

THIRTY-SEVEN

Clint got up, walked over, and sat down opposite Arnie Coleman.

"What do you want?" Coleman asked.

"I've got some questions for you, Coleman."

"What makes you think I'll answer any questions you have?"

"Because you know I didn't kill your boss."

"You're crazy—"

"No," Clint said. "That's why I wanted to talk to you over here, where nobody else can hear us. We both know I didn't kill Ed Kennedy."

Coleman thought a moment, then squinted.

"So who are you sayin' did it?"

"I think his wife had something to do with it," Clint said. "Barbara."

"What do you know about Barb—about Mrs. Kennedy?" Coleman demanded. He could see in the man's eyes that he was right, at least partially.

"I know she's a woman with appetites," Clint said. "Appetites her husband wasn't satisfying . . . so who was, Coleman?"

"What do you know—you don't know her!"

"Sure I do," Clint said. "I met her yesterday. Last night."

"What?"

"That's right," Clint said. "I got out of here while a deputy was looking down the front of a saloon girl's dress."

"You got out? What'd you do? And why the hell did you come back?"

"Yeah, you wish I'd kept going, right?" Clint said. "That would have proved I did it. But I didn't and we know it. She did, and she had help."

"You're crazy," Coleman said.

"You think so?" Clint asked. "Wait till I tell you where she went this morning."

"Where?"

"Over to the Triple R," Clint said.

"What the hell was she doin' there?" Coleman demanded.

"She saw Andy Rivers," Clint said. "Spent about forty minutes in the house with him."

"With the old man?" Coleman said. "Not Stark?"

"Stark came later," Clint said, "just after she left."

He'd watched Barbara ride away, had let her go. Then, as he was about to leave, Stark rode up.

Now he got it, especially with the look on Coleman's face.

"She rode out, Stark rode in," Clint said. "But they were both out there for a while. And look at you, worried that she was with Stark."

Coleman looked away.

"I get it," Clint said. "She can't be satisfied by one man. She had you and Stark going. But which one of you killed Kennedy?"

Coleman glared at Clint.

"I'd never kill Big Ed. Never."

"But you'd sleep with his wife, right?"

"If you met her," Coleman said, "then you know."

"So who did it, Coleman?" Clint asked. "Stark? Or did the lady shoot her husband herself?"

"I ain't sayin' anythin' against her!"

"Well, you're not going to frame me for this murder, Coleman," Clint said. "If it was you, I'll get you. Same for Stark. And the same goes for her. Think about it."

Coleman gave Clint a hard look, then it softened. He turned his head, then got up and walked out.

Clint went back to the game.

THIRTY-EIGHT

Clint sat down at the table again.

"You find out what you wanted?" Lawson asked.

"Would you believe me if I told you?" Clint asked.

"I would," the judge said.

"Me, too," the mayor said. He looked at Lawson. "After all, he did come back."

"Yeah, okay," Lawson said. "Go ahead."

Clint looked at Chambers, who nodded.

He told them what he had found out, what he thought, and what Coleman had told him. He didn't tell them about the night he'd spent with Barbara Kennedy.

"The young wife," the judge said, shaking his head. "What a surprise."

"But who'd she get to do it?" the mayor asked. "Coleman or Stark?"

"Stark's the gunman," Lawson said. "My money's on him."

"Your money was on me, too," Clint reminded him.

"Good point," the bookkeeper said.

The judge looked at Clint.

"What do you think?"

"I don't think Coleman did it," Clint said. "I think maybe she wanted him to, but he wouldn't."

"Then why didn't he warn his boss?" the judge asked.

"Because, in his way, he was being loyal to both of them."

"And that got Big Ed killed, right?" the mayor said.

"Apparently."

"So it was Stark?" the judge asked.

"Or her," Clint said. "I wouldn't put it past her to do it herself. The only thing I don't understand is, why did she go to Andy Rivers's ranch this morning?"

He'd figured out that it had to be Stark who had pinned him down, probably to give her time to get to Rivers's ranch. But what had she done once she got there?

"Rivers wouldn't have helped her," the judge said.

"Then her going to his ranch must have been just a ruse, to throw me off the trail."

Okay, now it made more sense. She'd gone out to meet Stark, and he knew Clint would be on her trail. So he sent her to Rivers, knowing Clint would follow. And he'd pinned Clint down long enough for her to get there. Only, why hadn't he just killed him?

Because Clint Adams was still the number one suspect.

"What do you plan to do?" Lawson asked.

"Well, that depends."

"On what?"

"On Coleman, for one. He's got to convince his men I didn't do it."

"Why would he do that?" Lawson asked.

"Because he knows I didn't. They're all acting on his word."

"Let's say that happens? Then what?"

"Then I'd have to confront Stark," Clint said. "He either did it or knows she did it."

"And he's gonna tell you?" the judge asked.

"I don't know."

"What if he tries to kill you?" Lawson asked.

"He had one chance, and he passed it up," Clint said. "The only way he'd try again is if he was sure I was in the clear. Then there'd be no reason to keep me alive. And dead they might still be able to pin the murder on me."

"Okay," the judge said, "then I'll tell Yatesman to have Coleman tell his men that you've been cleared."

"Coleman's gonna go along with that?" the mayor asked.

"He might," Clint said. "After I talked to him, he just might.

Yatesman was getting tired of being called in and sent out of the saloon. He liked it better when it was closed.

"Now what?" he asked the judge.

"I want you to go out and tell Coleman that Adams has been cleared."

"What?"

"That means he didn't do it," Lawson said.

"How do you know?" the sheriff asked.

"I'm the judge," the judge said. "I know things like that. Now go out and tell Coleman that Clint Adams did not kill his boss. And tell him to convince his men of that fact."

"Judge, this ain't right," Yatesman said. "I'm the sheriff, and I ain't cleared nobody."

"You haven't done much of anything, Sheriff," Lawson said. "Cleared or unclear."

"Fine," the lawman said, "you want him cleared, he's cleared. It ain't no skin off of my nose."

Yatesman stormed out.

"Now what?" the judge asked Clint.

"Now we sit back, play a few more hands," Clint said, "and wait."

THIRTY-NINE

When the sheriff delivered the news to Arnie Coleman the Bar K foreman did not react the way the lawman had expected.

"Well then," Coleman said, "I guess we better break this up."

"Just like that?" Yatesman asked. "You were so convinced he did it."

"Yeah, well . . ." Coleman said.

"What did Adams say to you inside?"

"Look, he got out of the saloon, and out of town, and he came back. If he did it, why didn't he just keep goin'?" Coleman asked.

"And that's enough to convince you?"

"Well, the judge has cleared him," Coleman said. "He's just about the smartest man in town. If he thinks Adams didn't do it . . ." Coleman shrugged again.

"Well, I gotta see if you can sell this to your men," Yatesman said.

"Oh, they'll do what I tell them to do," Coleman told him.

* * *

The men gathered and listened to what Coleman had to tell them.

"You're kiddin'," one of them said.

"No, I ain't."

"How could that be?" another man asked.

"The judge cleared him," Coleman said, "and I'm convinced he didn't do it."

"But you were so convinced he did!" another man said.

"We been out here for days!" still another man shouted.

"We're goin' home, men," Coleman said.

"To do what?" someone asked.

"To run the ranch," the foreman said.

"Is there gonna be a ranch?"

"That's what we're gonna go back and find out," Coleman said. "We're done here."

Many of the men milled about, still unconvinced, while others went to get their horses from the livery.

Coleman walked back to the sheriff.

"Tell the judge we're leavin'," he said.

"All your men agree?"

"I told you," Coleman said, "they'll do what I tell them to do."

"I don't get it, Arnie," Yatesman said. "What really convinced you?"

Coleman stared at the lawman. He couldn't very well tell him that he knew from the beginning that Clint Adams had not killed Ed Kennedy.

"Let's just say the Gunsmith and the judge are real convincing."

"Did they threaten you?"

"Nobody threatened me, Sheriff," Coleman said. "It's just over."

Coleman walked away from the sheriff toward the livery, with most of his men following him.

Yatesman wasn't convinced. He thought the Gunsmith and the judge must have come to some kind of arrangement. And he also thought his job was going to be in jeopardy, after this.

He looked up on the roof and saw that Coleman's kid was still up there with his rifle. Nobody had bothered to tell him it was over, and he was apparently too dumb to figure it out for himself. So Coleman would lead his men back to the Bar K, leaving that one up on the roof to take his first clear shot at Clint Adams.

Yatesman shrugged.

FORTY

Yatesman came back into the saloon.

"The Bar K boys are pullin' out," he said.

"Joby!" the judge shouted.

The boy came running.

"Yes, sir?"

"Take a look outside."

"Yes, sir."

Joby ran to the door and peered outside.

"Looks like their leavin', Judge," Joby said, "and they're takin' the bar down."

The judge looked at Clint.

"Now what?"

"Let's wait and see what happens when the word gets around," Clint said.

"You think the real killer will come after you, now?" Lawson asked.

"I don't know," Clint said. "Maybe the real killer will just leave."

"That would be like a confession," Lawson said. "Killin'

you would be better. Like you said, folks would never be sure if it was you or not."

"Well," Clint said, "we'll give it a few hours and then rest it out."

"How?" the judge asked.

"I'll just take a walk outside."

"You think that's wise?" the judge asked.

"Unless somebody's got a better idea."

Three hours later Sammy was standing with his elbows on the bar and his head in his hands. Three hours and no customers had returned, yet.

"Poor guy," Chambers said, looking over at the bartender.

"Don't worry," the judge said. "The customers will come back, if only to drink where the Gunsmith spent so much time."

"I'm flattered," Clint said. "Okay, gentlemen, last hand."

Sammy lifted his head and looked over at the table.

"Finally?" he asked, hopefully.

"Already?" Lawson asked.

"Looks to me like everybody here," Clint said, looking around the table, "could use a shave."

Parker Stark rode into town and immediately spotted the kid on the roof with the rifle. He'd been looking for an edge against Clint Adams and hadn't been able to find one. In the end he'd decided to just come in and face the man. After all, he was just a man.

But the rifle on the roof, maybe that would be the edge.

He reined his horse in, dismounted, and tied his animal off. He knew why he and Barbara Kennedy wanted the Gunsmith dead. That was the only way to keep him a suspect—forever.

But what was Andy Rivers's reason for wanting the man dead? Why would he be willing to pay so much?

He probably wouldn't get an answer to that, unless he survived.

He loosened his gun in his holster, took a deep breath, and started walking toward the center of town.

Charlie Hicks stared down at the street. What was going on? Where was everybody? They wouldn't have pulled out without telling him, so they must have all taken cover. That meant something was about to happen.

He picked up his rifle, leaned on the edge of the roof, and sighted down the barrel.

Then he saw Parker Stark walking down the street.

"Judge?"

"Yes, Joby?" the judge asked.

"There's a man walkin' down the street."

"Do you know him?"

"I think—wait . . ."

Clint took the final hand, raked in his pot, then looked over at Joby, who was staring out the saloon window.

"Yeah, Judge," Joby said, "it's that man who works for Mr. Rivers."

"Stark?"

"Yeah, Stark."

Clint moved his eyes around the table, came to rest on the judge.

"Gentlemen," he said, "Looks like it's time for me to step outside."

FORTY-ONE

Clint stood up and walked to the bar.

"Let me have a beer, Sammy."

The bartender drew him a beer and set it in front of him.

"You payin' for that?" he asked.

"Sure." Clint dropped the money on the bar, then picked up the beer. He held the beer up to the town council. "Gents, I can't wait to put this town behind me."

"I don't see why," Lawson said. "You got all our money."

"For the amount of money I made at your town council meeting," Clint said, "I don't think it was worth the aggravation of being suspected of murdering someone I never even met."

Clint drank down half the beer, set it back on the bar, turned, and went out the front door. The town council rose, en masse, and hurried to the front windows to watch the action.

Clint came out the batwings and saw Parker Stark standing in the street. He wondered where Sheriff Yatesman had gone to.

"Stark," he said.

"Adams."

"Any particular reason for this?"

Stark shrugged.

"Money, a woman, a reputation," Stark said. "Take your pick."

"I'm thinking all three. It helps that the woman has money."

"Ain't just the woman," Stark said. "My boss is payin' me for this."

"Why does Rivers want me dead?" Clint asked.

"Beats me," Stark said. "I'm just doin' what I'm paid to."

"Just answer me one question before we do this?" Clint asked.

"Go ahead."

"Why kill Ed Kennedy?"

"What? I didn't kill Kennedy."

"Then who did?"

"I thought everybody was sayin' you did."

Clint frowned.

"Okay, then, we've established neither one of us did it."

"What does it matter?" Stark asked. "Only one of us is walkin' away from here. If it's you, then you can go and find out who did it."

For a moment Clint wondered if he was wrong about Coleman. Could the foreman have killed his boss?

No, he still didn't think so.

Charlie Hicks stood and took aim with his rifle. Should he wait until after, or do it now? What if Stark killed Adams?

He decided to do it now.

"Charlie."

The kid turned, saw Arnie Coleman standing behind him.

"Arnie, I was just getting' ready to—"

"Time to go home, kid," Coleman said. "Come on, let's go."

"You sure?"

Coleman nodded. "Positive."

Hicks looked down at the two men in the street, then lowered his rifle and followed his boss off the roof.

"Okay," Stark said. When was the kid on the roof going to take his shot? he wondered. Was he waiting to see who was going to come out on top?

"Don't worry about the rifle on the roof, Stark," Clint said, as if reading the other man's mind.

Stark stole a look.

"He's gone."

Stark looked at Clint.

"Don't matter. I didn't put him there, anyway."

"But you were going to take advantage of him being there, weren't you?"

Stark shrugged.

"Everybody needs an edge."

Clint stepped down into the street.

"I don't," he said. "I just need my gun. See, if you're going to do this, you should be able to depend on your own gun and nothing else."

"Fine," Stark said, "let's do it, then."

"She's not worth it, you know," Clint said. "No woman is worth dying for."

Clint hadn't even said it to gain an edge, but that was how it worked out. The remark incensed Stark.

"You son of a—" he said, telegraphing his move badly.

But if he ever had a move he'd lost it since leaving south Texas. Clint took his time, drew, still showed first, putting a bullet in Stark's chest.

Out of nowhere, Sheriff Yatesman appeared. His gun holstered, he walked to Stark to check him.

"He's dead."

"Where were you?" Clint asked, ejecting his spent shell and replacing it before holstering his gun.

"I was watching."

"From a safe place?"

Yatesman shrugged.

The town council came out of the saloon.

"Yatesman," the judge said, "turn in your badge. You're fired."

Yatesman stared at each member of the board, then took off his badge and tossed it into the ground.

"Tell your deputies the same goes for them," the mayor said.

"You tell 'em," Yatesman said. "They ain't my deputies anymore."

He walked away.

"You better let at least one of those deputies hold on to his badge, Judge," Clint said. "You're going to need someone to make an arrest."

"Arrest? Who?"

"I'll let you know."

FORTY-TWO

Clint rode up to the ranch house and dismounted. The ranch hands eyed him from a safe distance, none of them willing to approach him. Clint looked around, then approached the front door and knocked. The door opened and they stared at each other.

"I figured you'd been cleared when all my men came back," she said. "Come in."

He entered, then followed her to the living room, where she sat down on the sofa. He chose a separate chair.

"You're angry with me," she said.

"Yes."

"Because I ran out on you?"

"You didn't run out on me," he said. "You ran to Parker Stark. Then you let me tail you to Andy Rivers's ranch, to make me think you had a relationship with him."

"I could have a relationship with him," she said. "All I'd have to do is say the word."

"You lied to me about Coleman, trying to make me think he killed your husband."

She didn't reply.

"That means that either you killed him yourself or you know who did and are protecting him."

"Stark—" she said.

"Stark's dead."

"You killed him?"

"Yes. He didn't give me a choice."

"Foolish," she said. "You men are foolish." She shook her head. "To face each other in the street."

"Some men face each other in the street," he said. "The ones with honor. Others will shoot men from hiding, shoot them in the back. Those are the cowards."

"You're all fools."

"You mean, we're fools for you, like I was? Like Stark was? And Coleman? Is Rivers one of your fools?"

She smiled.

"Not yet. Maybe never. I don't need his money. I have my own."

"You mean your husband's."

"Yes."

"Did you kill him, Barbara?" Clint asked. "Just between you and me. Did you kill your husband?"

"No," she said. "I didn't have to."

"Because you knew one of the men who wanted you would do it."

She didn't answer.

"So it was Stark, or Coleman, or Rivers, except that I believe Coleman that he didn't do it."

"Good," she said, "then I'll let him keep his job."

"And then there's Stark, but he's dead."

"So you'll never know if he did it."

"But I know something else," Clint said. "According to Stark, Rivers paid him to kill me."

"And you believe him?"

"Yes," he said, "I don't think he had any reason to lie to me."

"What about Matt Holmes?" she asked.

"He's the joker in the deck, I guess," Clint said. "But he doesn't have a gunman working for him, he's not after you . . . is he?"

"God, no," she said. "He's older than my husband was."

"And older than Rivers?"

"Yes." She went on.

"My husband was alone at home the day he was killed," she said. "The hands were all out working, and I . . ."

"You were with Parker Stark," Clint said. "You alibi him?"

"Yes."

"And nobody broke in?"

"No."

"Would your husband let someone like Holmes or Rivers in if they came to the door?"

"Sure he would," she said. "He'd never think either of them wanted to kill him. They were business rivals, but not enemies."

"As far as he knew."

"Yes."

"Okay, Barbara," Clint said. "I'm done here."

"Are you . . . sure you won't stay?" she asked, seductively.

"Positive," he said. "I won't play the fool for you again."

"Tell me you didn't enjoy it."

"I did enjoy it," he said, "I enjoyed the hell out of it, but I won't do it again, not after all the lies." He waved. "You have Coleman, or you have your pick out there. Now you enjoy."

"Clint—"

"Good-bye, Barbara."

Clint went out the front door, mounted Eclipse, and rode away.

FORTY-THREE

Clint made two more stops. The second, and last, was the Triple R ranch.

"Adams," Andy Rivers said, when he opened his door. "What are you doing here?"

"Expecting me to be dead, Rivers?" Clint asked. "Sorry to disappoint you, but it's your man Stark who's dead."

Rivers had the good grace to look disappointed.

"Yeah, he told me you hired him to kill me. What I want to know is why?"

Rivers stepped outside on the porch, looked out at his ranch.

"I was getting ready to lose all this, did you know that?"

"I had no idea," Clint said, and then thought, how would I?

"Big Ed Kennedy finally figured out a way to get it away from me," Rivers said.

"And he got Matt Holmes to go along, didn't he?"

"How did you know that?"

"I stopped to see Holmes before I came here," Clint said.

"He told me he was getting ready throw in with Kennedy against you. Do you know why he'd do that?"

"Sure. Matt and I have been working a long time at getting rid of Kennedy, and we couldn't do it. So they decided to go in together to get rid of me."

"So why would you kill Kennedy and not Holmes? He's the one who betrayed you."

"He didn't betray me," Rivers said. "We're not brothers. But Kennedy . . . he's the one who came here when Matt and I had the area split in two. With him gone we could go back to the way we were."

"So you just walked up to his door, knocked, caught him off guard, and shot him?"

"Easy as that," Rivers said. "Surprisingly easy. I'd never . . . killed anyone before. You believe that? Built all this without killing a soul."

"Until now."

Rivers nodded, looking old and tired. "Until now."

"What made you pin it on me?" Clint asked.

"I didn't mean to do that," he said. "I heard you were in town, just thought I'd pass the word that Ed was going to hire you."

"And let nature take its course, huh?"

"That was the general idea . . . I guess."

"Okay," Clint said, "let's get your horse."

"Taking me in?"

"It's the last thing I'm going to do before I leave this town behind me."

"You don't have to, you know."

"I know, but I want to make sure my name is cleared."

"I'll send word to town," Rivers said. "I'll clear it all up, but I'm asking one thing."

"What?"

"Don't take me in," he said. "I'll take care of it myself."

"Take care of it?"

"Here," Rivers said. "In my home. I'll write it all out and then . . ." He shrugged.

Clint knew what the look on his face and the shrug meant.

"Please?" Rivers said. "I know you don't owe me anything."

"No," Clint said, "I don't."

He went down the porch steps, mounted up, and rode away—away from the Triple R and away from Cannon City.

When the single shot came from the house, he was too far to hear it.

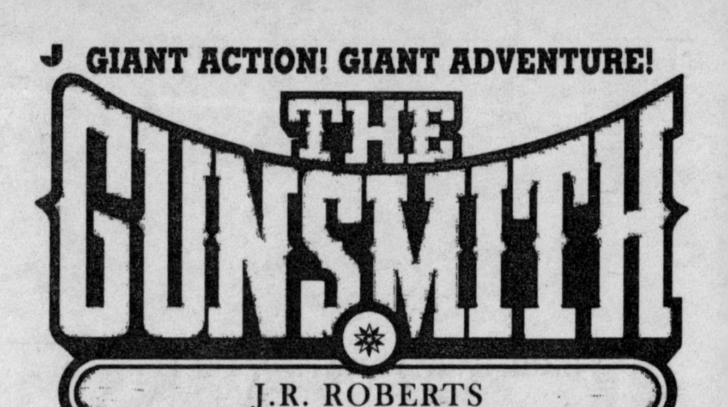

Little Sureshot And
The Wild West Show
(Gunsmith Giant #9)

Dead Weight
(Gunsmith Giant #10)

Red Mountain
(Gunsmith Giant #11)

The Knights of Misery
(Gunsmith Giant #12)

The Marshal from Paris
(Gunsmith Giant #13)

Lincoln's Revenge
(Gunsmith Giant #14)